Guilt Trip

Guilt Trip

Stephen Schwandt

ATHENEUM
NEW YORK
1990

Atheneum
Macmillan Publishing Company
866 Third Avenue, New York, NY 10022
Collier Macmillan Canada, Inc.
First Edition
Printed in the United States of America
Designed by Cathryn Aison
10 9 8 7 6 5 4 3 2 1

Library of Congress Cataloging-in-Publication Data
Schwandt, Stephen.
Guilt trip /Stephen Schwandt.—1st ed.   p.   cm.
Summary: High school junior Eddie thinks he may have found the solution to
his anger and unfocused identity in the beautiful, disturbing Angela Favor, until
she draws him into the investigation of the murder of her director at the
New Energy Theater Troupe.
ISBN 0-689-31557-0
[1. Mystery and detective stories.]   I. Title.
PZ7.S3995Gu 1990 [Fic]—dc20
89-15106 CIP AC

For Links

Guilt Trip

chapter I

The ice chunk fell against the accelerator pedal and the huge V-8 roared. The wheels, spinning, gripped the cold, dry asphalt of the service road, and the burgundy Cadillac fishtailed away, skidding over the hard-packed snow along the shoreline, jouncing onto the ice-covered waters of Lake Minnetonka. With its headlights off, the sedan soon disappeared in the frozen night blackness, barreling toward the weak spot and the deepest stretch of lake bottom.

In the car, the ex-theater director lay helpless. His hands and ankles were tied, his bleeding head lolling on the white leather seat. Barely conscious, blind and terrified, Corey wasn't sure what had happened, how they'd gotten to him at last. But they had him now. That was painfully obvious. He thought he'd recognized a few, but he couldn't be sure, and what did it matter? All he knew was, wherever they were sending him, he'd get there soon. The Caddy was picking up speed so quickly it pinned him back.

Dead ahead, directly in the path of the bolting DeVille, was the small tin ice-fishing shanty of bachelor, loner Emile Kozlicki, sixty-six, retired. Though it was late and cold, Kozlicki was there, inside, watching his lines, alone on the lake, warmed by his brandy and his kerosene heater. He was nearly halfway through still another action/suspense paperback, this one called *Gotcha!* by someone named Vassil Blue.

Emile Kozlicki was so absorbed in his reading, his fantasies, that he didn't hear the Cadillac until it was just ten yards from the fish house. With the book still in his hand, he leaned toward the peephole. He barely had time to raise his arms protectively when it hit, the Caddy smashing directly into the four-by-six shack. Before Emile Kozlicki could even scream, the fish house was bent nearly double and being banged along by the powerful sedan. Dizzy, gasping for air, Emile Kozlicki struggled to hang on while the DeVille kept churning toward the thin ice, the deep marked-off section of the thawing lake.

Inside the car, the ex-director had felt the force of the blast, taking still another painful blow to his head, probably the knockout punch. Corey was ready to give up now, ready to surrender. It was hopeless. Time to quit. No more time to think about it, pray for a break. No time at all.

For no sooner had he resigned himself to death than he felt the first cold shock. The Cadillac plunged through the ice, nose-dived, threw him off the seat and under the dash with head-splitting impact.

Abruptly, all motion ceased. All seemed suspended, held in weightless, momentary check. Finally the quick sinking began, the bone-deep chill, the fatal freeze, a last half breath before paralysis.

But then there was a sudden, surprising warmth. A warm, golden glow enveloped him and fast became intense. The shimmering light was not solid, more a misty presence, a bright, swirling fog. Corey knew there was something else, something beyond the humming golden glow, and he was anxious to see it.

In the next instant, plummeting wildly now, he melted, dispersed, floated, felt the most pleasurable sensation he'd ever known, far more satisfying than the obsessive pleasures he'd sought and found in life. He felt blessed, complete. Exquisitely stylized symphonic harmonies echoed inside his head as the car sank deeper and deeper, pushing down Emile Kozlicki and his shanty with it. Seconds later, all sensation ceased.

That moonless night, a late winter storm blew in, dropping nine inches of snow and covering the Caddy's tracks. The howling wind heaved up banks of snow and ice on the lake. The wind-whipped snow sealed weak spots, fissures, created others, and blurred the landscape, obliterating the death scene, hiding for now all traces of the crime.

chapter 2

"Edrich Lymurek," said the short, balding, and sloppily dressed teacher, pronouncing the last name "Limerick."

"Ly-MUR-ek," Eddie said, thinking, Here we go . . . *again*. His fifth school in only three years, and no one had pronounced it right yet on a first try. If the pattern and odds held, he figured he would attend several other senior high schools before graduating, if he ever graduated, and he'd have to correct teachers many more times. But you had to at least make sure they called you by the *right name*.

"Ly-MUR-ek," the guy repeated.

What was his name? Eddie wondered, glancing at his schedule card. Yeah, Goldman, social studies.

"Is it Ed? Rick? Rich?" Goldman asked pleasantly, staring over his half glasses and tapping his bearded chin with his pen.

"Edrich," said Eddie.

Goldman nodded, remained silent. "You know," he said at last, "I like Limerick better. It's got rhythm. And hints of rhyme. Which alla us white boys can use, of course."

Trying for a laugh, thought Eddie.

And he got it. Four or five black guys in back guffawed loudly, but not offensively.

Eddie tried to remain expressionless, cold-staring the teacher, giving him his best game face. This was an awkward situation. It was fourth quarter. These people knew each other. The class chemistry was mixed and Eddie felt painfully conspicuous, the outside element threatening the formula.

"So," Goldman continued, "that's what I call you? Edrich?" He wanted confirmation.

"Call me anything but late for dinner," Eddie popped, deadpan.

The black guys whooped half a second before everyone else. Even Goldman smiled. Eddie still hadn't.

Goldman allowed a pause and seemed to study Eddie. Then he asked, "Are you a case, Mr. Limerick? A problem child?"

"Peace child," Eddie replied softly, with a lisp.

"I see," said Goldman, nodding. "Well, glad you're joining us . . . whoever you are." He smiled again before pulling his lecture notes from his tattered briefcase.

* * *

At the end of the hour, on his way out, Eddie noticed a girl watching him. She seemed to be waiting for him.

"You're new, huh," she said when he passed by her.

He stopped, faced her. She wasn't too bad. Kind of shabby/classy, he thought, like a lot of city kids. Her hair was black and straight and hung to her shoulders. Her high forehead brought attention to her clear blue eyes and straight nose. Her inviting smile seemed to change in a hundred little ways as Eddie watched her, each subtle shift perfectly controlled. And she was wearing a *dress*, soft orange summer cotton with a scoop neck and a sash waist. It perfectly complemented her tan arms, shoulders, and legs. The careless-rich tropical look with maybe a touch of the artist thrown in.

That was it. Probably into *studio art*, painting freaky rock concert scenes, throwing intentionally lopsided pots. Then he thought he recognized her but didn't say so. Instead he replied, "I'm brand-new."

"You did okay with Moses in there. He can be really sarcastic. But he backed off you faster than I've ever seen. You must know something."

Eddie shrugged. "Moses?"

"Mo Goldman. Our teacher."

"Mm."

"Where're you from?" she asked.

"I was at Parker this winter."

"Oooooo, suburban boy."

"Not really." Eddie gave her a stony sideways look.

"So you know it already."

"What?"

"That Minneapolis Nicollet ain't remotely Parker."

"Yeah, I know it."

"We've got 'diversity.' You see all the diversity here?" she said, nodding toward three girls in leather, their heads nearly shaven, the remaining hair dyed flat black or bright white, one with her hand halfway down the back of her boyfriend's jeans.

"Uh-huh. Diversity," said Eddie.

"What I'm thinking," she continued, "you let your hair grow a little, color it darker, you could pass for Tom Cruise."

"Then I'd be somebody."

She smiled at that. "You could be an actor," she said.

That's when he definitely placed her. And she saw it.

"You remember me now?" she asked.

"From auditions," said Eddie.

"Uh-huh. Not that long ago."

"You've changed," Eddie said lamely. Thinking maybe her hair was longer now.

"You haven't," she said. "You still pop off."

That comment reminded Eddie of his brief entanglement in the world of NETT, the New Energy Theater Troupe. Early last year a school psychologist had urged Eddie's dad to get his son into drama as a way of dealing with his "hyperactivity and unfocused identity." Bobby Lymurek had been told that working with the NETT might prove "the ideal haven of sublimation" for Eddie, if only he could get involved in a play. Eddie was immediately intrigued by the idea of the theater. NETT was well known in the region. Actors there got into the news. Eddie found he liked the thought of being on stage, up front for real, finally seen and heard. Maybe it would provide a chance . . .

On his own, with no help from his dad, Eddie had badgered a secretary into giving him a tryout. But after preparing for a week, he blew his audition in the first two minutes.

The confrontation had started predictably enough. When Eddie walked out onto the brightly lit thrust stage, the senior director, who was sitting high in the balcony, shrouded in shadow, said, "You're . . . Edrich Lymurek?" He, too, pronounced Eddie's name "Limerick."

Eddie corrected him. "It's Ly-MUR-ek."

The director answered with sarcasm. "Oh, *of course*," he said. "I should have *known*." Then, "Have you prepared anything?"

Eddie held up a script of *Juvie*, the one-act being cast that day. He said, "I'm going to do Skip's monologue, the one at the beginning."

"I've read the play, too," scoffed the director. "But thanks for the help."

Low, mocking laughter echoed from the darkness behind the director.

Eddie asked, "Should I start?"

A disturbing pause followed.

"You've never done this kind of thing before," said the director.

"No. No, I haven't."

"Just anybody off the street can do this?"

Eddie chose to remain silent, giving the guy a puzzled look, waiting to see where he was going.

"Okay, listen. This play demands a bit more than routine memorization and . . . primitive posturing. We need people who can . . . *improvise*, play it all the way out when it gets a little tricky."

Again, Eddie heard young laughter from the dark balcony.

"Are you with me?" asked the director.

Eddie held his pose, staring unblinking at the shadowy figure, the caustic voice. Even though he was suspicious and feeling defensive, Eddie risked a small nod.

"Very well, then," continued the director. "Let's try a piece of spontaneous enactment. Why don't you pretend you're a kernel of popcorn just as it explodes into a nice, white, puffy treat."

With that line, the sniggers from the balcony became guffaws.

Eddie had stood quietly a few seconds more, hands on his hips. He glanced away, then brought his gaze back to the director and said, "Why don't I do a fruitcake being eaten by a fruitcake?"

This time a collective gasp from the wings led to nervous laughter. When the laughing stopped, the disembodied balcony voice called out, "Next!"

Instead of leaving the stage, Eddie said, "There's no popcorn in this play." He waved the script at the director.

"*Next!*" yelled the voice again.

"Listen, man," Eddie continued, raising his voice, "I *walked* all the way over here, okay? And I've read this thing *ten times*! Just let me do the scene."

"Remove him from the stage!" hollered the director, still obscured by the shadows.

Eddie looked to his left and saw two burly stagehands in jeans and T-shirts coming at him. He smiled and raised his arms, palms out. He said, "Be cool, I'm goin'."

The stagehands stopped short. Eddie headed off in the opposite direction. But instead of taking the narrow passage leading to the stairs, he walked right into a wall of scenery that pictured a small-town storefront. Eddie then fisted and chopped his way through the tempera-painted display window.

Behind him he heard the stagehands running. As he raced for the stairs, Eddie could hear the director bellowing, "Let him go, *goddammit*! Let him go! Next! Next!! *Next!!*"

So he got away.

During his walk home that afternoon, Eddie had shifted between rage and depression. He'd only wanted a chance to compete at NETT, to win a place for himself there and belong to something important and interesting. But once again he'd lost out before the game even began. He'd let his temper get between himself and what he wanted.

"I remember Corey messed up your name, too," the girl said, pulling him back into the conversation. "You really got him mad that day."

Before Eddie could respond, describe for her how

mad *he'd* gotten, the bell rang, making the girl go wide-eyed, say "Dammit!" and run off down the hall, clutching her books to her chest.

As she disappeared around the first corner, Eddie realized he'd never gotten her name. He couldn't remember if he'd ever known it. But he did recollect that as he was hurrying out of the NETT complex after his non-audition, this same girl had said, "Be happy, you're clean." Something like that. Eddie had had no idea what she meant.

He smiled now. She wasn't half bad. Maybe things would turn out pretty good all around. She had some brains, anyway, and a sense of humor. But that she cared about getting to class on time, that bothered him. He shook his head and calmly went into his act, staring vacantly at his schedule card till a vice-principal spotted him, came over, and said, "You lost?"

"Guess so," Eddie said, waiting for the directions to his next class, which was only a few doors away. He had his first-day routine *down*, knew how to milk passing time for all it was worth, cut class hours in half sometimes, all without penalty. Sometimes it was okay to be new . . . and odd.

On his way to second hour, though, Eddie began thinking this might be the toughest transition of all, going fourth quarter, junior year, from an uppity-yuppity suburban "academy" to an old ragtag city school that seemed to house anything on two legs. Which he rather liked, actually. And to be around a school like this in spring might be especially okay. More kids felt like taking chances in spring, having a little fun.

Whether he remained at Nicollet for the entire quarter depended most on how well he could get along with ACE, his aunt Cynthia Edrich, who was, he'd concluded, pretty strange. She typically made him feel out of it. She was just past forty but still always ready to try something new.

They'd had a few frank talks by now. She'd told him why being married years ago hadn't "agreed with" her. "I understood very quickly how I'd lied to myself, thinking I needed and wanted that kind of structure, all that security," she had said. "I lied and hurt someone I admired very much, and I promised myself I'd never do either again, if I could help it."

Since then the ACE had become so independent she wouldn't even let a career shackle her. Whenever she chose to reveal her smarts on the job, and the bosses came running at her with promotion offers and added responsibilities, she'd quit on the spot. Whenever she felt threatened or controlled, she simply withdrew from the competition.

Lately, she'd been making a nice living at her own speed, in her own home, on her own terms, doing some free-lance magazine writing and lots of beautiful artwork. Most of the jewelry, bowls, and plates she made involved an enamel-on-copper method she seemed to have perfected and personalized.

With Eddie, she'd even been honest enough to confess to "poly-drug use" during her younger years, "from twenty to forty," she joked. That's when she warned him that real freedom wasn't possible without rigid self-discipline. "You get into bad chemistry, Eddie, you're begging to be a victim," she said. And those were her last words on that subject.

As for parenting, she once said to him, "Your life hasn't been very stable, has it." That, they both knew, was a monumental understatement. For Eddie's life hadn't been stable *at all*, except as defined by the pattern of his father's mood swings.

Bobby Lymurek was described by his buddies as "one helluva salesman." He sold sporting equipment, repping for several large companies. During the two years that Bobby had spent at the university on a football scholarship, "Batterin' Bob" had been "one helluva running back." Until the game when his right knee blew out. Then he became one helluva quitter, leaving football, school, and sobriety behind. "Sure, he gets a little knocked once in a while," another of Bobby's pals said to Eddie late one night. "But what the hell, a guy gets bored."

Naturally, thought Eddie. That explains everything.

Everything for Eddie began when Bobby married Eddie's mother—already pregnant with Eddie—and then left her when Eddie was barely old enough to remember him. Eddie had lived with his mother until she remarried and decided that Eddie didn't fit into her plans anymore either. She'd had it pretty tough, Eddie realized that, and now she had a chance to travel and indulge herself for the first time in her life, so she grabbed the opportunity. He couldn't really blame her.

Eddie spent his next years following his dad from marriage to divorce to "relationship" to marriage to divorce to *new love*—"It's the real thing this time, kid."—

to divorce again, until finally Eddie couldn't take it anymore, because all during these upheavals, he had experienced a series of smaller, even more personal ones.

The pattern was, whenever his father had made up his mind to get out of one marriage and into another, he would manufacture vicious arguments over some imagined or petty failure on Eddie's part: "I told you to clean the damn garage *carefully*, like you actually had some pride in what you're doing! Look at this! I mean, if you can't even sweep out a goddamn garage, what the hell else can't you do?"

When Eddie made the inevitable mistake of talking back, the dispute exploded into an all-or-nothing confrontation that invariably ended with Eddie's getting kicked out of the house. He was then taken in by a succession of sympathetic relatives—uncles, cousins, even a former stepmother. Aunt Cyn, his mother's sister, was Eddie's best hope by far.

Sooner or later, after all these episodes, Eddie would get a call from his dad, once Bobby Lymurek was settled in again and feeling secure. He'd offer to give Eddie another chance and Eddie had always gone back. But this time he knew he wouldn't, couldn't possibly. If he failed to make a go of it with ACE, he would simply have to make it on his own somehow. And that's what bothered him most about both his parents—neither one of them ever stood up for him. They never showed him *how* to stand up. They took care of themselves first and left Eddie to hang on any way he could.

Amazingly, almost no one at any of the schools Eddie had attended knew much about his home life. And

Eddie did his best to diffuse curiosity about himself by maintaining what he called his "Clyde Cool" perspective. And a good part of that involved his self-image as a basketball player, a poised, competitive *talent*. Bobby had never forgiven him for that decision either, choosing basketball over football as his sport.

So after school, having made it through all his classes in a trance, Eddie was looking for a game. He shuffled out of the building with *everybody*. Place should be called Interfaith Camp, thought Eddie, all races and creeds, shapes and sizes.

He was halfway across the parking lot when he spotted some action at the far end. He headed toward the asphalt court, thinking about how he'd really messed up basketball this year. Late in the season he'd managed to get himself dropped from the program at Parker for "breaking team rules."

When he reached courtside, Eddie saw that all the players but one, including the odd man out standing next to him, were black. The white kid was a wiry center, at least six foot six, who could really jump.

"Shoot hoops?" asked the black sub without looking at Eddie.

Even in jeans, a T-shirt, and ragged running shoes Eddie thought, Yeah, I belong.

"Uh-huh," said Eddie.

"Willis!" the guy called. "Boy here say, '*Play me!*' "

The game stopped, and everyone looked at Eddie, checking him out.

"Heyyyyy," said one of them. Eddie assumed it was Willis. "It's you, man. Ol' Call-Me-Anything."

Eddie smiled, nodded, knew Willis must be in his social studies class.

"Yeah. *Limerick*," said another.

"C'mon, white bread. See what you got," said Willis jovially.

"An' what you *don't* got," added someone else, a deep voice, Eddie couldn't see whose.

"Aw, be nice, Alex," said Willis.

Then turning to the lone white player, Willis said, "Okay with you, Birch?"

The guy glanced at Eddie, shrugged, and said, "Why not?"

"You don't be guardin' each other, now," teased Willis. "We want some integration here."

The quip got Willis a healthy laugh.

Willis smiled at Eddie. "You know Birch?" he asked.

Eddie shook his head.

"Man, I thought alla you guys knew each other."

The black players laughed again.

Eddie asked, "Birch, that's your name?"

"Nickname," replied the rangy redhead. "Real name's Karl Werner."

"Okay," said Eddie. "I'll remember that."

Werner shrugged, turned away, and joined his teammates.

The game was now four-on-four, full court. Eddie played guard. There was only one guy smaller than he was. This had to be the TEAM, thought Eddie, the Nicollet varsity. He hadn't paid much attention to the city conference this year, but these guys were all big, strong, and quick.

On the first series, Eddie's man, dribbling, tried to take him baseline. Eddie beat him to the spot and the guy charged him, knocked him back into the basket support. The dribbler stopped half a second, glowered at Eddie, then continued in for the lay-up.

"Call it, man!" hollered one of Eddie's teammates.

"C'mon," said Eddie, his hand out for the ball, his man within reaching distance.

"You bleedin'?" asked the dribbler, pretending to examine him for wounds.

"Yeah, okay," said Eddie. "I get it."

"Ain't dumb," said the guy, shoulder muscles rippling. He tossed Eddie the ball and headed downcourt. Eddie passed in, not caring that the basket counted, knowing they'd let him play a little longer because he wasn't a whiner.

And he definitely wanted to keep playing. The game made the most sense here, with the guys patrolling each other, having control over themselves. It was when the coaches and referees and parents and other adult egomaniacs got involved, trying to control everything, that's when the game went directly to hell. So Eddie liked street ball because it seemed more honest.

As soon as they were all downcourt, Eddie went up for a free-throw line jumper. Then he spotted one of his forwards cutting along the baseline, his arm up, finger pointing at the basket. Instead of shooting, Eddie lofted a perfectly placed ally-oop pass that the swing man caught one-handed and jammed.

"*Pretty!*" said the dunker as he ran by Eddie.

The game went to twenty baskets and Eddie did okay, scoring three times, checking his man effectively on defense, not embarrassing himself too much. The other team won, however.

Afterward, while they rested on the sidelines, Willis said, "Don't remember you in the league."

"I was at Parker."

"Starter out there?"

"For a while."

"Yeah? Then what?"

". . . It didn't work out."

"Why?"

"The coach."

"Yeah," said Willis guardedly. "Ain't it always."

Eddie looked at the ground.

"Your name again."

It wasn't a question. It was an order.

"Eddie. Eddie Lymurek."

"What's that 'Edrich' jive?"

"You were in the back."

"With the brothers."

"Your choice? The back row?"

"Uh-huh. Goldie know how to get along."

"Well, it's Eddie, okay?"

"Fast Eddie, man. Fast Eddie Limerick. Sound like a rock star."

"Or a *pimp*," said the intimidating forward from the other team. He glared at Eddie, then wandered off, moving back onto the court.

"That's Alex," said Willis. "He's prejudice."

"Oh," said Eddie, unsure of himself suddenly, seeing Alex hadn't broken into a big friendly grin of acceptance. This is no joke, thought Eddie.

"You remember that," said Alex, over his shoulder.

"He serious?" Eddie asked Willis.

"Uh-huh. White boy hurt his brother real bad last year. Cops couldn't touch 'im either."

"Why not?"

"Some damn thing, I don't remember 'xactly. Bought a good lawyer, I guess."

Eddie didn't ask for any more details, didn't want to seem too anxious or shocked. He looked to Birch for support, clarification, but Karl Werner shook his head and looked off.

"Well, gotta split," said Willis. "See ya."

"Sure," said Eddie, sneaking another glance at Alex, watching him go toward the street with the other players. Willis left then, jogging to catch up to the group. Eddie checked around for Birch, but he'd already disappeared.

"They like you."

A girl's voice, right behind him.

Eddie turned and there she was again, the tropical sweetheart wanting a Tom Cruise look-alike. He walked over to her.

"You're pretty good," she said. "I like basketball players. They're as close to their audience as jocks can get."

He smiled, fixed on her eyes. "That's an interesting attitude," Eddie said.

"I'm Angela Favor," she said, smiling back. "And I'm an interesting girl."

"Yeah," said Eddie.

"You got a car?" she asked, looking around.

"Not today," Eddie answered, as though tomorrow he'd have one—fat chance.

"Me either."

A silence built before she said, "Guess I'll walk."

"Where?"

"Home."

"Ride the bus."

"I don't feel like it."

Eddie nodded, had no idea where to take the conversation next.

"You live close?" he finally asked.

She pointed vaguely and said, "Near Lake Harriet."

"Sort of on my way," said Eddie. "I'll walk with you."

"A mind reader," she said.

It wasn't until the last few steps of their twenty-block trip that Eddie discovered Angela Favor didn't quite live near Lake Harriet. She lived in a sprawling Tudor mansion right *on* Lake Harriet.

Across the steet, actually, but *so what*.

chapter 3

Angela was surprised to find the front door unlocked. She poked her head in and took a quick breath. Her father was home. Thank God she'd sent Eddie for a walk.

"Well, well," muttered her father, standing there, swishing around the last of his "drink," rattling the ice cubes. Angela knew it was a fake and that once again he was just practicing. Her father attended lots of parties where deals were cut for huge sums—with huge fees— and he liked to have an edge over his sloshed competitors. So he'd invented half-a-dozen look-alike drinks that were nonalcoholic but didn't smell that way. And he'd walked out of those parties with all the best accounts.

"You coming or going?" he asked, breaking the pleasant silence.

Angela kept her eyes averted and stepped into the house, easing the door shut behind her.

"Where'd you get that one?" he said.

She looked up and saw her father nodding toward the front window. She understood then that he'd been watching her . . . with Eddie. How unusual, she thought. He'd noticed.

"He just walked me home is all."

"So you've truly given up on affirmative action?" he replied, staring out the window.

Angela said nothing.

"He isn't much, judging from appearances, but he does represent an effort on your part"—he stopped to stifle a belch, then continued—"an effort on your part to ascend the ladder of human development."

Angry now and growing tighter by the second, Angela caught herself, realized just in time that she had to play this scene out carefully. She mustn't show her strength, not yet. She remained silent.

Her father, she knew, would *never* miss an opportunity to express his feelings about her dating Adrian— Adrian, who was so bright . . . and black. Especially considering how it ended. She had wanted a scene then, something that would royally embarrass her father. But things had gotten out of hand. She'd lost control that time. So right now, the last thing she wanted to hear about was Adrian.

She'd recently gone through a "sass" stage with her father and discovered that arguing, defending herself, was far more degrading than simply putting up with a relatively good-natured tease like today's. For he, her father, was R. Todd Favor, Mr. Big Bucks corporate attorney, who loved more than anything to win expensive arguments and be financially and socially revered for doing so.

"That's a compliment," he said, resuming the confrontation.

"Why're you home?" she asked.

"I live here, remember? I own it."

"It's only four o'clock," she persisted.

"I've got to pick up some things for your mother. She's meeting me downtown. Dinner and a benefit performance."

"So you'll be home pretty late."

"Whenever," he said.

She sensed a chance to get away, so she turned toward the stairs.

"Where do you think you're going?" he said.

She stopped but didn't face him.

"I asked you a question."

"To my room," she replied.

"I meant tonight, obviously. You seem rather anxious to have us gone. That guy out there your next?"

"I've got rehearsal," she said evenly, facing her father. "Remember?" She was mimicking him but not dramatically enough for R. Todd to notice.

He pursed his lips, cleared his throat, put down his empty glass, grimaced, and said, "Whatever."

Again, Angela started to retreat. More than anything right now she wanted the assuring silence of her room. But before she could walk away from him he said, "Be home by ten-thirty."

"If we're done rehearsing by then," she replied.

"*Be* done," he said.

She did not respond. She knew from experience that precisely at ten-thirty her father would call, just to catch her being defiant.

She also knew he didn't care anymore about what she did, giving her all the leeway in the world, but not really. He was actually on some weird power trip, behaving like those duds she dated, the guys who wanted to appear so cool when they knew she liked them that they would ignore her, never even look at her in school, but then become jealous, possessive little dictators if she decided to look at someone else. That was her dad, acting like he didn't want her to go out at all, ever, but just stay home and be Daddy's girl. In truth, she missed those little-girl days and knew she'd been looking for them ever since.

Things hadn't always been like they were now, all tense and angry. Her father was once very different, very personal and caring toward her. But that was before he went from being sort of rich to being very, very rich. And that was before she started seeing boys and staying out late and doing whatever he thought she did that drove him away from her. That was before Kevin and Adrian and . . . Corey.

"Ten-thirty," he repeated, startling her. Then he turned his back and disappeared down the hall that led to the garage.

Angela swallowed the parting shot she wanted to fire at him and started up the steps. She thought, He can't even *imagine* asking if I need a ride to the theater. He wouldn't care if I ran off with the Vice Lords, so long as I didn't mark up *his* buildings with graffiti. She reached the top of the staircase just as the back door banged shut. That's when she remembered Eddie Limerick.

Eddie had taken the long way around, not circling the block as Angela suggested, but circling four square blocks. Specifically, she'd told him to "go float" while she checked out the house, made sure no one was home. He tried walking slowly, but his mind, his imagination, was racing, starting to run away. If all this were real, he couldn't believe his good luck. And on the first day of school. She wasn't just funny and smart and nice looking, but *rich*. The girl had it made.

Eddie was about to turn onto Angela's street when another thought hit him—the paranoid possibility that maybe this wasn't the girl's house after all, that it *was* too good to be true, that maybe she's into some daredevil break-in number and wants ol' pseudoinnocent Eddie along to bolster her nerve. He didn't know where the idea came from, probably some bad movie he'd seen. Maybe his suspicious nature. He kept walking.

About the time his fear fantasies were becoming vague, he caught a glimpse of the big dove gray Mercedes sedan just as it began backing out of Angela's driveway. Eddie slipped behind some tall lilac bushes and waited for the car to disappear. He tried to sneak a look at the driver, but the windows were tinted so dark that Eddie couldn't see a thing. When the car was gone, he came out of the bushes and approached the house.

He was passing the front walk when he heard her voice.

"Looking for something?" she said, peeking around the brick wall guarding the grounds.

"Always looking," Eddie answered. "Who was that?"

". . . Nobody," she said.

"*Nobody* in a Mercedes?"

"Okay, my father."

"What's okay about him?" joked Eddie.

"He's gone."

"Oh."

"Shall we?" she said smiling now, gesturing toward the monstrous house.

Inside Eddie went slack jawed. He'd never seen anything like it in real life. It was even more impressive than the mansions he'd gawked at in movies.

"What's he do, this father?"

"He never loses," she replied, looking off.

"Never loses what?"

"Listen," she said, facing Eddie squarely now, "could we just talk about something else?"

"Absolutely. What're *you* all about?" he said. "Let's start there."

She took his hand, pulled him gently toward the stairway.

"C'mon," she said. "Let me show you."

Together they scaled the stairs and followed a wide, dark corridor past room after room, stopping finally at a door that opened into a corner suite at the back of the house.

"My boudoir," she said softly, pushing the high solid wood door all the way open.

What Eddie saw made him marvel all the more. The room was enormous, nearly a small apartment, with a sleeping area, large desk built into a wall lined floor-to-ceiling with bookshelves, a sitting area with a small TV and even a minirefrigerator.

"Who all lives here?" asked Eddie.

"Where?" she answered, puzzled. "In the house?"

"In this room."

She laughed. "It is a bit excessive, isn't it."

Eddie looked at her, asked, "Where'd that come from?"

"What?"

" 'It is a bit excessive.' You really embarrassed by this, or just showing off?"

She waited a moment before answering, maybe trying to figure out if Eddie was kidding her or being real sarcastic, criticizing her. Then she asked, "Are you rich?"

"No," he said. "I'm not rich."

"Neither am I," she declared.

"Well, somebody is."

"Daddy. I told you."

"And you're the heir apparent, right? So what? Be

glad you've got all this to look forward to, or fall back on. That's how I see it. You can't possibly lose with this much help."

"You don't think you have to put up with anything, living like this?"

"Nothing I couldn't handle."

"Don't like it if you haven't tried it, okay?"

"Why not?"

"Look, you're talking to someone who's had all the security and structure and advice she can take, the best that money can buy."

Eddie didn't know what to say. So he looked around again and on the opposite wall discovered a collection of theater programs pinned up in neat, precise rows. Above the display was a banner that read: LIFE IS PERFORMING!! THE REST IS JUST WAITING AROUND.

"You've made it big lots of ways," he commented. "I mean since the last time I saw you."

"I've finally gotten some leads. I worked hard for every one, too."

"I believe it."

"But they don't mean as much now. The competition's pretty weak, not like when Corey was there."

"The actors aren't as good?"

"Lots of good ones dropped out."

Eddie faced Angela again and found her staring at him, her lips parted. In the two-beat silence that followed, Eddie knew this was a special girl . . . and a special place . . . and a special moment.

"I didn't always live here," she said, holding Eddie's eyes with her gaze.

"Oh yeah?" He took a step closer.

"We were out in Edina awhile, but my father grew up in the city and always dreamed of living in a place like this."

Eddie took another step toward Angela.

"Only Daddy didn't realize when he bought this, not everybody respects private property."

"You've had break-ins?" asked Eddie, moving even closer.

"Two," she said.

Eddie was next to her now and he put his hands on her bare shoulders. He thought it was a nice easy move, not too serious or pushy. What he didn't want was to get caught standing around, watching his chance slip away. So he winged it, still far from being experienced enough in these matters to know for sure if he was making exactly the right move, or if any move was right. The sky was the limit, for all he knew. Or maybe the limit was warm, smooth, bare shoulders.

"You're wondering why I want you here," she said, looking at his chest.

"It crossed my mind just now," he replied, his tongue suddenly awkward, surprisingly thick in his mouth.

"I don't know why," she said matter-of-factly, shrugging out of his light grip, turning her back to him.

"Maybe you are showing off," he said. "And that's okay," he added. "I'd do it, if I lived here."

"It's just that I remembered you, the way you didn't put up with anything that time at auditions. And I was glad to see you again, glad to see you made it. And I felt lonely." She swung around and faced him again. "Okay?"

"Whatever," Eddie replied, smiling and wondering what she meant by *made it*.

"Don't say that."

"Don't say what?"

" 'Whatever.' I hate that. It sounds like you don't care about who you're talking to or what's being said."

"Sorry," he offered. Then, "You've got some very definite opinions. I guess that's good, right?"

"And please don't patronize me."

Eddie stared at her. "You know what?" he said. "I'm never sure what that means, patronize."

"Talk down to."

"I was trying to lighten things up a little. I'm glad to see you, too."

Suddenly, she was right in front of him again, rising on her toes this time to kiss him. He put his arms around her and brought her close, wanting to make it last. But she eased back and brought her hands up to his face, touching him gently. "Let's be friends," she said.

"What—"

She cut him off by putting her finger on his lips.

"To friendship, then," said Eddie, looking for another kiss. But again, Angela slid out of the embrace. She took a step back and gave him an appraising look, like saying, My oh my. Eddie didn't know what to think.

Then she said, "I've got to get ready for rehearsal."

"And you don't want to lead me on."

"I'm not a tease, no. You'll see."

30

"But for now I'm dismissed."

"Cut it out, okay?"

"You know what I think?" said Eddie. "I think you're a good girl who wants to try being a bad girl." Even as he talked, Eddie was asking himself, Where do I get these garbagy grade-C lines?

Angela said, "Don't think so much."

"But I'm right?"

"And if you can't think better, don't *say* too much either."

". . . Pardon me," muttered Eddie, hurt but not willing to show it.

"It isn't personal," she said ambiguously.

"So there's still friendship," he said. "And I should take what I can get."

"That's how it works. In life, I mean."

Eddie asked, "Are you happy?"

"Are you?"

"If we can be friends."

"Don't hang too much on that. People let you down all the time."

"You keep bubbling with optimism, I won't be able to tear myself away," Eddie said.

"You're right. I'm getting negative and morbid. That always happens to me just before big rehearsals."

"Well, have a good one. I'll go if you want."

"To rehearsal?"

"No, no. I meant home. But I'd like to see you work sometime, if that's all right."

"Sure. It'd really be okay tonight, especially if you had a car."

"You don't have one here?" he asked, genuinely amazed.

"It's being fixed. I'll get a ride with somebody. Don't worry."

"Wish I could help," said Eddie. Then he remembered that ACE had wanted him home by four-thirty for some special reason, and he knew he was already hopelessly late. "I gotta run, too," he said, and started for the door.

"You're not going to try to kiss me again?" she asked.

Eddie looked over at her. She stood a little straighter, arched her back.

"It's a risk," he said, smiling.

"No guts, no glory," she said.

Eddie took a quick breath and half a step toward Angela when she said, "Shhhhhh! Listen!" Then, "Dammit, *now* who's home?" She went for the far window and peeked out. "Wouldn't you know," she said, letting the curtain drop.

"Who?" asked Eddie, leaning closer, wanting a look.

"My cousin Tom. He works for my father. He's probably playing gofer again, something he can handle."

"What should I do?"

"Go out the front door. He'll come in the back way. He's got keys to the place. You better hustle. I'll see you tomorrow."

"At school."

"Where else?"

"Just making sure," he said. "See, I'm going for perfect attendance this quarter, the gold star."

* * *

When Eddie finally walked into his aunt Cyn's Victorian duplex, he was ridiculously late for supper. He found her sitting in her study, reading.

"Hi," he said.

She looked up, not smiling, but not scowling either.

"So how was your first day of school?" she asked with mild sarcasm.

"The usual," Eddie replied.

Later, after Eddie had made himself some soup and a sandwich, ACE said what she had to say.

"Eddie," she called, from her study.

"Yeah?"

"Come here."

Eddie closed his eyes, shook his head, walked through the rooms, knowing what was coming. He'd screwed up already. He quickly found himself facing Cynthia, standing in the arched doorway of her study. The day's last sunlight streaking through the tall windows made the room glow. She was at her rolltop desk typing.

"You called?" he asked, trying to change the mood.

Without looking up she said, "I don't like announcing rules. I like repeating them even less. I try to deal with situations and problems as they develop. And we've got a situation here." She finally looked at him, frowning. Her thick, prematurely gray hair glittered in the shafts of sunlight. "Don't we?"

"A situation?" asked Eddie.

"Don't we have a misunderstanding that merits immediate attention?"

"Sorry," he said automatically, looking at the tips of his shoes.

"For what?" she asked.

"Being late for supper."

She observed him a moment before continuing. "I like to think I know you a little," she said.

"You do."

"I know you need more room than most, but I'm responsible here. And that's not something I'm used to. And I'm not sure I like it very much."

"You want me out, just say so. I understand."

"I want what you want."

"What's that?"

"I guess we have to decide. Talk about it, communicate, that's the least we can do. Be honest, keep each other informed."

Eddie didn't know what to say. He gazed at his aunt Cyn with respect. She was a tough one.

"Eddie, you know you'll have to do worse than miss supper to get the toss from me. But I bet if you try, if you really concentrate, you could think of a way to alienate even your favorite aunt."

"I'm afraid so."

"Me, too."

"Anyway . . ."

"What I'm saying is, I didn't take you in so I could pretend to be a mommy or because I'm dying for company or because I want somebody around my little kingdom to say 'Yes, ma'am' whenever I want to hear it. I'm doing this as a favor to the Universe, the Cosmic Imagination. Because there's a spark of it in all of us. In you especially."

Eddie grinned a slow grin, not sure of Cynthia's meaning, not even sure of her tone. Was she serious?

"You, Eddie," she continued, "are ablaze with imagination. That's what scares me about you. Everyone I've ever known who's been that way became frustrated, then angry, then self-destructive. I don't want that for you. So if I can help, I will."

"As a favor to the Universe."

She laughed. "I think we can understand each other. Don't you?"

"Yes, ma'am," said Eddie, bowing.

Later that evening they both sat munching popcorn, absorbed in the ten o'clock report, watching the vivid color footage of the police wrecker as it dragged a burgundy Cadillac DeVille and the dead ex-director, Corey Howe-Browne, out of the water and onto the shore of Lake Minnetonka's Smith Bay.

chapter 4

The next morning, during first hour, Eddie listened to Goldman's lecture and wondered when he'd get to see Angela again. He'd looked for her before school but had no luck. And she wasn't in class. Eddie's mind drifted.

Suddenly his daze was broken by, "Mr. Limerick, for or against?"

"Huh?" Eddie mumbled as laughter rippled across the back of the room.

"For or against, Mr. Limerick," Goldman repeated, his face expressionless, his eyes flat, all business.

"It's Ly-MUR-ek," said Eddie, feeling the blood rush to his ears. He didn't want any more teasing attention from Goldman. He wanted now to find a place in the class, fit in, build some security for himself.

"For or against," Goldman said again, still completely deadpan.

"For or against what?" Eddie asked quietly.

"Let me simplify," said Goldman even more softly. "For or against *freedom*."

Eddie's eyes narrowed with suspicion. "For," he replied. "Totally."

"Who agrees?" asked Goldman loudly, scanning the class. "A show of hands."

Everyone voted with Eddie.

"Okay," Goldman concluded. "Unanimous." He let a few seconds of strained silence pass before adding, "Then how, in all seriousness, can you sit there and accept what our big strong country is doing to lots of little weak countries throughout the world?"

"Ahhh, current events time," whispered somebody behind Eddie.

Willis said, "Goldie lookin' for the heavy rap."

And they were right, both of them, for Goldman quickly launched into a period-long lambasting of America's foreign policy, the militaristic meddling, the propping up of right-wing dictators. His presentation left nearly all of the class confused and challenged, confused about whom to believe and challenged to learn the truth.

"What I'm saying is, we've lost something," concluded Goldman. "And that something is a sense of community, a commitment to the common good *worldwide*. We've lost our sense of moral, social responsibility. We're being told now that our best move in life is to get ours while we can and get away clean with it. After all, we're the Ship of State, right? We roam the Third World, wander from port to port, taking on supplies, ripping off the little guys because we've got to stay afloat, right? Right?"

The bell ending the hour rang, yet everyone remained seated, waiting for Goldman to give them assurances, some hope that things could be better. Instead he finished with a shrug, said, "So? Whaddaya gonna do?" And waved them out.

Angela was there to meet Eddie, standing against a row of lockers halfway down the hall. Eddie hurried toward her.

"I was looking for you," he began. "Before school."

"I should hope so," she said, winking. "But I just got here."

"Sleeping in? What about Goldman?"

"I switched to another hour, got a first-period study hall instead. I always do that fourth quarter."

"And you'll attend it faithfully."

"Oh, sure."

"Will I ever see you here before nine?"

"Probably not," Angela said. "Rehearsals. They're getting later and later."

"Working hard."

"Uh-huh. What'd he talk about?" she asked, nodding at Goldman's room. "Everyone looks so depressed."

"American diplomatic history," Eddie replied. "What a crock it is."

"That'd do it, depress anybody."

"So," Eddie continued, "you watch the news last night?"

"This morning."

"What was he doing there, in the lake?"

"Corey Howe-Browne?"

"Who else?"

"How should I know?"

Suddenly Eddie broke into a big smile.

"What's funny?"

Eddie said, "Howe-Browne now cow."

"Huh?"

"Howe-Browne now cow."

"I heard you. The hell does that mean?"

"You know, that old line, 'How now brown—' "

"I mean," she cut in, "why's that funny?"

"I just imagined myself saying it to him, your director."

"And?" she asked, frowning.

"And he didn't laugh either."

She laughed then, tilting her head to the side, narrowing her eyes, appraising him. "You're crazy," she said. "I like that in a guy. I can work with that. And you'll appreciate me."

"I do already," Eddie answered.

"I mean for something that's really important."

Eddie asked, "You think it was suicide?"

"Maybe," said Angela. "Corey was supposed to go to jail. Everybody hoped he'd get ripped apart there."

"Who's everybody?"

"All of us who were *had*," said Angela, her eyes angry.

"And *everybody* remembers what he did," commented Eddie. "Typical saturation coverage. Freedom of the press."

"Of course."

"Did you know about him and the boys before the story broke?"

"Sure. Everybody knew."

"And nobody complained?"

"A couple times, when it got really bad. He was having them up in the control room, during rehearsals even, *doing things*."

"Didn't the girls? . . ." Eddie let the question hang there.

"The girls," answered Angela, her face fiercely taut, "were ignored completely."

"Mm."

"Hey look, I just thought of something. If you're not busy tonight, why not come to rehearsal with me. It'll be okay and maybe you'll enjoy it. Openness is the new byword over there. All observers welcome. You can even watch some of the victims."

"They're still in it?" Eddie commented. "After what's happened?"

"What else can they do? Some of them are real veterans, kid actors for most of their kid lives. Full-time students at the school. Only a few couldn't handle it and had to quit, but not that many."

"Were you ever full-time?"

"My first season, three years ago. A therapist convinced my father NETT would save me."

"From what?"

"Myself, I guess," she answered sarcastically. "I've been in weekend classes ever since."

"Why didn't you stay full-time?" asked Eddie. "I mean, how can you keep up with the others?"

"I know what I'm doing, and I like diversity, remember?"

Eddie smiled. "Oh yeah," he said.

"Actually I needed a break from the place. I put enough pressure on myself to improve. I didn't need the NETT coaches on my case all day every day to . . . *live the theatah!*" she said with a sweep of her arm.

"I guess not," said Eddie with a grin.

"So?" she asked.

"So . . ."

"So will you come tonight?"

"I'll see what I can—"

The bell cut off Eddie in midsentence.

"No!" yelped Angela, grabbing Eddie's wrist, glancing at his watch. She spun away from him and disappeared quickly around a corner.

"Bye," he said, reaching in his back pocket for his schedule slip. He stood there scratching his head until the same vice-principal approached him.

The V.P. said, "Mister, weren't you here yesterday?"

"Dunno. Maybe," mumbled Eddie, trying to sound spaced, and succeeding at it.

The V.P. frowned, stepped closer. He seemed a lot bigger today, at least two hundred pounds. "Now get this, mister," he said, "I *saw* you trying to charm the young lady."

Eddie stared at him through half-lidded eyes.

"You better be more careful . . . starting right now."

Eddie stood passively in the awkward silence that followed. He was waiting for the V.P. to issue the late slip, give him an hour's detention after school. But the man ended it with a warning. "If I catch you again playing games, you'll owe me time, lots of it."

Eddie nodded, said nothing.

With that the V.P. walked off. He'd gone three or four steps before calling back over his shoulder, "You've got ten seconds."

Eddie took off for English class, the room just down the hall, only six seconds away. And already he knew this was not a subject to get kicked out of. It was a perfect spring activity—"Mythology for the Masses." That was the course title. And from what Eddie could tell, the class was simply a film festival. The teacher, a dozy string bean named Pakorney, was content to spend his career showing all the B movie remakes of the great Greek legends.

Yesterday, when the film had ended and Pakorney flipped on the lights, he looked over his mostly comatose students and remarked, "I think we're losing cabin pressure."

My kinda guy, thought Eddie.

That night at rehearsal, Eddie watched transfixed in the stunning, modernistic New Energy Theater Troupe Auditorium as Angela, playing Rosalind, breezed through several scenes from *As You Like It*. The play was to be NETT's featured offering over the summer.

From his back row seat, Eddie had no trouble following the development of the scenes, but given the recent history of the theater, he winced when the character Orlando practiced for his wooing of Rosalind with a "boy" who was actually Rosalind in disguise.

Afterward, Eddie met Angela in the lobby. He asked her about the choice of plays, considering the delicacy of the situation.

"Howe-Browne picked it," she said. "And the budget for it was approved and all the scenery and costume work optioned out. So they couldn't just drop it. Cost them a fortune."

Eddie recalled what he'd learned about Shakespeare as a sophomore. About how all Elizabethan actors were men and boys, and how boys took the girls' parts. So that in Shakespeare's time a boy would have been playing a woman (Rosalind) who in turn played a boy being wooed in the play by a man and . . .

"Howe-Browne had a confused worldview," said Eddie.

Angela, looking away, replied, "Yeah. Oh, yeah." Then, looking warmly at Eddie, "I'd like to ask you over again."

"But . . ."

"But they're home. And, you know, it's late. . . ."

With that, Eddie jerked up his wrist, stared at his watch. "Geez," he said, amazed.

"You in trouble?"

"Nahhh," Eddie concluded. "For a change." And they walked out to cross the brightly lit parking lot.

chapter 5

Eddie arrived back at the duplex and found the rooms dim, the only light coming from Aunt Cynthia's reading lamp. She was curled up on the couch, absorbed in a mystery.

"How was it?" she asked Eddie.

"Interesting."

"Who is she?" Cyn gave him a smirk. "This girl you'd go to the theater for."

"Hey, c'mon now. I like the theater, pretty much. Always have."

"Who?" interrupted Cynthia, making a little rolling gesture with her hand as if to say, get on with it—talk.

"Her name's Angela Favor."

Cynthia's eyes opened wide. "Rrrrrreally," she purred. "You do go right to the penthouse, Eddie."

"What's that mean?" he asked, wondering if ACE was commenting on Angela's reputation as an actress, or a poor little rich girl.

"I mean she's one of the best they have. I've seen her perform three or four times. She's always effective, even in minor roles."

"I guess," said Eddie, relieved. "Tonight it was Shakespeare, *As You Like It*."

"For summer stock?"

"Right. You *do* know the game."

"I've got season tickets, have had for years."

"Small world."

"And getting smaller. What'd she say about Corey Howe-Browne?"

"Not much. She pointed out some of his conquests, but they looked pretty normal to me."

"Eddie, they *are* normal. Howe-Browne's the irresponsible one. They believed in him, in his talent, and he took advantage."

"Intro to psych," Eddie said, snapping his fingers, then pointing at Cyn.

"Uh-huh," answered Cynthia with a smile. "And if pushed, I can still spew psycho-babble with the best of 'em."

"But you're right, though. I can see that."

"How'd she get along with him?"

"She resents the way he ignored the girls. He never featured them."

"That's true. In fact, I can't remember a single play where . . ." Cynthia closed her eyes, suddenly lost in thought.

"What is it?" asked Eddie.

"Some of the girls had their own exploiters," said Cynthia, meeting Eddie's gaze. "Did you know that?"

"She didn't mention it," he said. "Guys on the staff?"

"Yes."

Eddie said nothing.

"Well, I hope they left her alone. It'd give me another reason to hate that board of directors, their inattentiveness."

Again, Eddie made no comment.

"It was on the news tonight," Cynthia continued. "Howe-Browne's getting more publicity for his antics than he ever did for his artistry."

"What now? Anything new?"

"Lots. Plenty. Like the police refuse to call it a suicide or some kind of accident."

"Really?"

"What time is it?" she asked abruptly.

Eddie glanced at his watch. "You noticed I'm home early?"

"Turn on the TV. There's bound to be more."

Cynthia and Eddie listened carefully as a reporter "on location in front of Roger Doyle's comfortable Kenwood home" attempted to interview an obviously hostile subject. Mr. Doyle, a tall, sandy-haired, good-looking man in his early forties, stood before the ornately carved front door as though he were guarding the house. The reporter, an aggressive young woman with a beautiful face, remained a step below him and had to reach awkwardly up with the mike to catch his responses.

"I'm getting tired of this," Doyle was saying.

"Then of course you know of Mr. Howe-Browne's death?" the reporter asked.

"Only what you guys are splashing across the screen every waking hour. What is it, ratings week?"

"You were particularly vocal during Mr. Howe-Browne's trial, isn't that right?"

Doyle glowered at the reporter. "I testified," he said finally.

"Wasn't it a little more than that?"

"Look, I'm not the least bit sorry for anything I said. As far as I'm concerned, the guy lost his humanity—any right to live around other people—when he did what he did. And I don't feel the least bit upset he's dead. I won't lose a second's sleep over it."

"You're probably aware, too, that the police aren't willing to call it an accident. They supposedly have information implicating people connected with NETT, including parents. They think—"

"I don't care what *they think!*" snapped Mr. Doyle. "What *I think* is you'd be smart to get off my front steps. Or I'll call for assistance." Doyle smiled condescendingly, then quickly disappeared inside the house.

The reporter, facing the camera now, standing down on the sidewalk before the imposing house, continued, "Roger Doyle, you may recall, was perhaps the most outspoken parent at Corey Howe-Browne's trial last July."

"That's neat," Eddie commented.

"What's neat?"

"How she just brought this guy's kid into the conversation without ever referring to him directly."

"Yes," Cynthia replied, staring now at an old videotape of Doyle, dressed in a suit and tie, being interviewed as he left the courtroom.

"No!" he barked at whoever had asked him a question. "A goddam slap on the wrist is what he got. This creep has ruined lives, and all he gets is a few months in the workhouse, a year of 'required therapy'? That's *obscene*! But it's not over, tell you that much. He'll get—" Doyle cut himself off and shouldered his way though the crowd as other journalists shouted questions at him.

"That," said the young woman on Doyle's sidewalk, "was Roger Doyle last summer, immediately after the sentencing of Corey Howe-Browne for sexual misconduct.

"What makes Roger Doyle's anger and frustration, as well as that of other NETT parents, so relevant now is the refusal by police to call the death a suicide. Earlier, we talked to some of Mr. Howe-Browne's friends and associates about that issue."

The scene then changed to the front steps of the NETT school, where a thin, balding man in his late twenties, dressed in sandals, jeans, and a work shirt, was speculating from behind wire-rimmed glasses.

"When Corey disappeared last winter," he was saying, "we were positive he simply left town. The thought of jail was truly anathema to him." The man looked at the reporter and suddenly broke into a self-conscious laugh that he kept up for too long. The reporter made no comment, just held the mike in his face.

"What's funny?" asked Eddie.

"Shhh," Cyn replied.

"He wasn't suicidal," the man continued, serious again. "He wasn't behaving in any way like a man ready to kill himself."

"Could you explain that statement?" asked the reporter.

"The patterns, you know."

"Which, exactly?"

"Oh, giving away prized possessions, depression, drug abuse, withdrawal, threats. Corey wasn't like that at all. Actually, he came out of this mess in good spirits. He wanted to put it behind him. And he was very excited about some possibilities of getting theatrical work."

"What a guy," said Eddie. "Mr. Fresh Start."

"Actually, the night he vanished he was supposed to join a group of us for a concert at Orchestra Hall."

"Did you report him missing when he didn't meet you?"

"Uh . . . no."

"Why not?"

"Because . . ." The man looked pleadingly at the reporter but said no more.

"Can you remember the exact date of that concert, the one Mr. Howe-Browne failed to attend?"

"Yes. It was March fifteenth."

The camera cut back to Roger Doyle's front steps. There the reporter continued with, "While the police refuse to speculate publicly about the circumstances surrounding the death of Corey Howe-Browne, an informed source has revealed that Howe-Browne's hands and feet had been tied, bound with a very special kind of rope. It's called Shur-Go hemp, and it's used almost exclusively by specialized landscapers to hold burlap around the root systems of certain mature trees during transport. It's a rope that's supposed to dissolve when wet, thus enabling the roots to spread and take fairly quickly. In Mr. Howe-Browne's case, not all the Shur-Go dissolved. Roger Doyle is founder and president of Landscape Design Statements."

"Bombs away," mumbled Eddie.

That night in the Doyle home, fourteen-year-old Tom Doyle lay wide awake in his second-story bedroom. His door was open, and he could hear his father's angry replies to the police investigator's questions. The detective was a big black guy, very tough. Every now and then Tommy heard Richard Kaplan, his father's attorney, throw in a few comments, his voice sounding calm but very firm.

Then Tom heard his dad yell, "I told you. I'm glad he's dead, all right? But if I were the lucky one who did it, would I be so stupid? Hell, I hope not."

"Mr. Doyle," said the detective, who was amazingly patient, "we're only trying to explore some possible—"

"I know what you're trying to do," cut in Doyle. "You're trying to get a quick score at my expense."

"That seems true, Detective," added Kaplan. "You appear ready to rely on *extremely* circumstantial evidence.

Anybody could get hold of enough Shur-Go to tie up Howe-Browne. It's not some kind of controlled building material or something. So what's the point?"

"The point," said the detective, "is we're pretty sure he was murdered. And I'm going to look at everything and everybody ever involved with this. *Anybody*."

It was quiet for a little while. Then Tommy heard the detective say, "Mr. Doyle, we know you had tickets for the same concert Mr. Howe-Browne was to attend."

Roger Doyle said nothing.

"That's true, isn't it?" asked the detective.

"That's what I hear."

"You bought the tickets?"

"No."

"I don't understand."

"They were sent to us, came in the mail. Some kind of promo deal, I think."

"Promo deal for what?"

"I don't remember. But I didn't buy the tickets. That's what you asked, and the answer is no."

"Did you attend the concert?"

"No."

"Why not?"

"We were on the way, my wife and I. Then we started talking. We needed to talk, be alone. We just drove around and talked."

"About what?"

"What do you think?"

"I don't know. That's why I'm asking."

"What that creep had done to our lives, my boy's especially."

"So you drove around for what, two or three hours?"

"I guess so."

"Mr. Doyle, there was a big snowstorm that night."

An uncomfortable silence built before Doyle said, "Actually, we decided at the last second to attend a meeting."

"Which is it? Did you drive or meet?"

"Neither."

"Mr. Doyle . . ." The detective's tone was suddenly ominous. "Stop dancing around," he said.

The guy has great voice control, thought Tommy, and projection.

Then Mr. Kaplan said, "Maybe we should stop now, Mr. Crenshaw. I think you're trying to intimidate my client."

"Mr. Doyle?" prompted the detective, seeming to ignore Mr. Kaplan.

Tommy listened carefully to his father's reply: "We went to the house where the meeting was supposed to take place, but no one was there."

"Who were you going to meet?"

"Other parents, NETT parents."

"Whose house?"

"Ed Russo's."

"He called you or something?"

"We got a card that afternoon."

"And you didn't call him, ask for details?"

"Like I said, we weren't planning to go at all until the last minute."

"Uh-huh," said the detective, Crenshaw. "By the

way, did you know those parents had tickets for the same Orchestra Hall concert?"

"No. Which parents exactly?"

"John Harrison, Trevor Caine, Edward Russo—"

"No way," cut in Roger Doyle.

Tommy, sitting up now, listened for more, but the voices faded. They were very soft for a few moments, Mr. Kaplan's being the loudest. Then they all moved off into the front hall, heading for the door.

He wished he hadn't heard anything. He knew he'd have another sleepless night. He hadn't slept well since they'd found Corey. So instead of sleeping, Tom Doyle lay there thinking—it wasn't supposed to end that way. It wasn't.

chapter 6

They came and got them right in the middle of practice, the middle of a scene!"

"Got who?" asked Eddie.

"Corey's boys."

"The victims?" Eddie replied as he walked Angela to her first-hour study hall.

"Everybody knew why, something to do with the killing."

"They interviewed one of the dads on the news."

"Which one?"

"Doyle?"

"Tommy Doyle's father," said Angela. "What'd he say?"

"Told 'em to get off his back. It looked like they

were trying to accuse him of something. Showed footage where he made threats last summer."

"Nice. Real fair."

"Where's the kid go to school?"

"He's full-time at NETT."

"Still?"

"Uh-huh."

"Why?"

"He's one of those guys, that's all he's got going."

"Dad didn't seem like the theater type."

"You never know."

"Did you know," Goldman asked, beginning the hour, "there's research strongly suggesting that Hitler could find, *with ease*, enough people in any American city of thirty thousand to staff all his death camps?"

Eddie raised his eyebrows and formed a silent *wow* with his lips. He wasn't being facetious.

"That's how intimidated people are by authority. That's why it's easy to find people who can be used, who are perfectly willing to bury their heads rather than choose the hard way, the responsible way."

"You authority, Mr. Goldman," said Willis from the deep corner.

"Good point. Am I? Or am I really a guerrilla freedom fighter, trying to lead you to enlightened independence of thought and behavior?"

"Can't tell most days," replied Willis.

Goldman laughed, very thin—ha, ha, ha. Then he

stopped, looked carefully at Willis, and said, "You like me, don't you? I mean, I'm okay, right?"

Eddie became suddenly alert, sensing that Goldman was really taking his chances with this discussion.

"Like you *how*, 'xactly?" answered Willis, inspiring cackles and giggles.

"Like me as an authority figure. I'm a nice okay authority figure. Not too much pressure, not too much hassle. You know?"

"You okay, sure. By me anyhow. Can't speak for alla us."

" 'Absolute power corrupts absolutely.' Ever hear that one, Willis?"

"Uh-uh."

"You want to know something that scares me?" Goldman asked, addressing the entire class. "Just think of all the people who are allowing horrible things to be done in their names because they've been morally drugged by some attractive or pleasant authority figure, someone who makes life seem easy and simple—some father type who inspires participation in his illusions. I mean, do we really want to vaporize the Russians, and ourselves? Do we really want to fund some dictator's death squad because we've been told he's a 'friend of democracy'?"

"Worth thinkin' about," said Willis.

"You bet it is," Goldman responded, not smiling.

The discussion continued for the rest of the hour, nearly everyone contributing something, making this class like no other Eddie had ever taken. Goldman really worked hard all period and made them work hard, too.

In just fifty minutes, Eddie confronted all kinds of ideas about the justifiable range of authority, its need for limits, the point at which it becomes exploitative rather than protective and nurturing.

With about five minutes left in the hour, Goldman ended the discussion and took a single sheet from his lectern.

"Before you leave, I'm supposed to read this." Goldman scanned the paper. "Looks like a public service announcement," he clarified. "It's that time of year again. These are the new fire drill procedures."

The class groaned.

"C'mon, man," grumbled Willis.

"Now wait," continued Goldman. "Listen carefully. Some of these changes are significant. For example, from now on when you hear the alarm sound, the first thing you're to do is buddy up, it says here. 'Don't panic and buddy up.'"

"*Sheeeee-uh* . . . get real, man," muttered a back rower, maybe Alex.

"So look around now," Goldman said, "and pick a buddy, someone you trust, and realize that whenever one of the vice-principals—in your case, Mr. Carlucci—blows his whistle, you should grab your buddy's hand and raise it high, so Carlucci can be sure everyone's accounted for."

"*Sheeeee-uh* . . ." said Alex again, loud enough for Eddie to hear, not Goldman.

"You serious?" Willis asked.

"Absolutely," answered Goldman. "May I go on?"

"My guest."

"Then, as you leave the building, look for a line of

those iridescent orange highway cones. They'll be set up in a circle around the entire school, one hundred fifty feet from the building. You're to go beyond the cone line and wait there for further instructions from Mr. Carlucci. When Mr. Carlucci appears with his bullhorn and orders you to 'assume the position'—"

The whole group erupted in laughter.

"This is no joke, people," said Goldman, all business. The class quickly came to order. "As I was saying, when the buddies are told to 'assume the position,' one of you must drop down on your haunches and hug your knees. Then the other buddy drapes himself or herself over you."

Goldman looked up, stared at the ceiling a moment, finally said, "I guess the theory is, should the place explode and spread lots of debris, at least half of you might come back alive so classes could continue."

Again, Goldman faced a barrage of raucous hoots.

"There's a corollary comment here," he said as the noise dwindled. "It says: 'Same-sex buddying will not be viewed with suspicion.' "

"Oh, gimme a very big break," said Krissy Klugel in her small, breathy voice. "Really!"

Goldman continued. "Now, in addition to the fire drill regulations, you should also be aware of the new look our tornado drills are going to have. For example, you all remember how crowded it is when we pack you into the basement during one of those exercises. Some kids actually do panic because they're claustrophobic or self-conscious or . . . elitist. Well, this year, to keep you people calm and give you something constructive to do with your emotions, we'll be handing out song sheets with antitornado lyrics put to some of your favorite pop tunes."

"No way, Goldie, no way," concluded Willis.

"So let's practice, huh? Right now! When the bell rings, pretend it's the fire alarm. Remember—don't panic, buddy up, and file out carefully."

Goldman had no sooner finished than the bell sounded. Immediately, people grabbed for buddies, laughing and joking but doing it just the same.

Eddie watched Goldman, heard him say, "Ahhh, Adolf, I see what you mean. Human nature you knew."

Eddie left class feeling challenged in the best possible way. Goldman had hit him where he lived.

After school, Eddie played in another pickup game. This time Willis and Alex and Bernard and Tyrone and the others beat on him a little less. Of the three games they played to twenty baskets, Eddie was on the winning side twice.

When the last game ended, all but Willis and Alex left. Willis sat down on the grass with Eddie, who was sprawled, exhausted. Alex kept shooting, practicing a little baseline move he'd messed up in the final game.

Willis said, "So it's you an' the Angel, huh."

"Angela?"

"She different, man. A ways off your beaten path. Got these ideas, you know?"

"Yeah?"

"You know?"

Eddie gave Willis a questioning look.

"You don't know," Willis concluded.

"Ideas like what?"

"You know, she be talkin' sometime, an' all at once she say like, 'My art *does* your life, baby.' You know, stuff like that, lotta jive, you know?"

"I guess."

"She ever lay that on ya?"

"Not yet, uh-uh."

"It'll come. She a strange one all right."

"What else?"

"You know . . . one minute she strut around like she thinkin' 'Boy, ain't I what's happenin'!' Then she go into a *thing*, man, an' don't talk for a week. Sometime when she talk, you can't tell if she be real smart or real stupid or real spaced out."

"You know her pretty good?" asked Eddie, staring over at Alex, watching him drill jumper after jumper.

"Nobody know her pretty good. Girl's too busy."

"Nobody?"

"Ain't for lacka effort neither. Speakin' from experience, you know?"

"Uh-huh."

"What she tell you?"

"Not much."

There was a pause before Willis surprised Eddie with, "Alex's brother Adrian, he tried gettin' close to her."

"Uh-huh," Eddie answered, on full alert now, unsure of where to go with the comment.

Willis looked off, seemed to let the subject drop, and a tense silence began to lengthen.

Eddie, more than a little nervous now, shifted his gaze back to Alex.

Willis turned to Eddie, said, "Can be dangerous with the Angel, man. Alex, he got a thing for her, too."

Eddie swallowed hard.

Later, at Cynthia's duplex, with supper cooking, the two of them watched the evening news, the latest installment in the ongoing drama of Corey Howe-Browne.

"He not only helped to found the New Energy Theater Troupe, but brought it to national prominence. At its peak, the NETT school boasted a full-time enrollment of over three hundred performing arts students. Now let's hear from interim NETT Director, Lawrence Ward, appointed right after Howe-Browne's arrest last year."

"The tragedy of Mr. Howe-Browne's life is that his many pioneering contributions will be dismissed and forgotten in light of his personal problems and now his death. In fact, this latest crisis seems to be threatening the very existence of the troupe itself. The months since his conviction have been very, very strenuous. Enrollment and endowments have dropped. Some fine faculty have resigned. So all the bad publicity is killing us, too," Ward ended ironically.

The camera cut from Mr. Ward to a handsome, dark-haired male reporter who closed with, "Mr. Corey Howe-Browne will be cremated tomorrow."

Eddie said, "Now they're talking like we've just lost

a great man. The last time he was news everyone on the story looked like they'd just stepped in a pile of doggy doo."

Cynthia laughed. Then she quickly turned serious. "Lots of artists have been condemned by conventional society," she said.

"But this guy was a sicko. By anyone's standards."

"It's not a simple situation."

chapter 7

Robert Crenshaw looked in the men's room mirror. He adjusted his tie and said to himself, "You gotta sweetheart now." He was referring to the Howe-Browne case, which he'd been put in charge of because it "needed creative perspective." What that meant was Crenshaw had just been stuck with the challenge of cleaning up a mess that got messier every time he asked a question.

Howe-Browne . . . Crenshaw mused, still gazing in the mirror, staring now at his tired eyes. How ironic, he thought. *The question*, he recalled, when he was first offered the detective/homicide job some years ago, was not *how brown* is Crenshaw, but how black? Hounded by affirmative-action lobbyists, the selection committee had decided to hire someone Very Black . . . Very Convincingly Black.

Not that Crenshaw didn't deserve the promotion. He probably should have had it years before. But that was life in the Nordic Northland. Crenshaw, however, wasn't bitter. He was realistic. He knew he could make it in Minneapolis about as easily as anyplace else. Since nothing would come easily to him anywhere, he thought, why not be a pioneer? The first black detective in the Twin Cities.

Crenshaw had been the first black many times in his life. He was the first black to be admitted to Forrest Prep High School in Houston, Texas. He was there because he was very smart but also very big and very fast. His football and track records at Forrest "would stand for a century," they'd said at graduation. Now, just as he'd done in college, grad school, and the academy, Crenshaw had worked his way into what had been another exclusive club.

Under pressure, he'd performed exceptionally well. He gained status quickly in the department by breaking two previous cases that had stymied everyone else assigned to them. In both situations, Crenshaw had *talked* his way to solutions. He closed in on his suspects and treated them like big-time athletic recruits. He'd be around them all the time, dropping in anyplace they might be hanging out, talking to them incessantly, showing them a little more of what he had, until *they* made a decision. If they ran, he pursued. If they offered to negotiate, he usually refused, pointing out instead their social and moral responsibilities, mesmerizing them with his deep, smooth, soothing voice. Several times he had extracted full, unqualified, attorney-witnessed confessions.

So when the precinct captain saddled with the initial investigation began sensing the complexity of the Howe-Browne problem, he decided to call Crenshaw. And that led to the tired eyes Robert looked at now. Already he'd been harangued by two irate fathers of victims who both wished *they'd* killed Howe-Browne and given themselves something to be proud of. Crenshaw had questioned the victims, too, and come away sensing that the NETT was maybe the most screwed-up collection of people ever gathered in one place for a common purpose.

But at least now he had a toehold, and he was determined to improve his footing and proceed. While his primary suspects were obvious according to all the cues found in Howe-Browne's burgundy Cadillac, what troubled Crenshaw was the world of difference between clues and cues.

Clues, of course, stand out in a murder scene because they don't always belong where they're found. *Cues*, on the other hand, are calling cards, items so obviously out of place that their discovery is no accident but part of a lucid design. Basically, Howe-Browne's car was cluttered with cues.

Crenshaw had already confronted Roger Doyle about the Shur-Go hemp and come away with little for his efforts. Even less productive was his challenge of Edward (Edwardo) Russo, the megabucks restaurateur, NETT benefactor, and NETT parent who, like Doyle, had been captured on videotape at Howe-Browne's trial memorably describing how he'd like to "flay Corey alive for what he's done to NETT." A steak knife (very sharp) bearing the Russo trademark was also found in the car, stabbed to the hilt in the passenger's seat. Russo had answered Crenshaw's speculations by saying, "Whole lotta bull . . . *Detective*. People lift those knives all the time. Anyone could've put it there. Maybe Corey put it there himself, just to throw something at me while he took care of business."

"What business?" asked Crenshaw.

"Suicide," answered Russo with a little smile. "His only option, really."

Tough guy, Crenshaw had thought, with his electric-tan face, slicked-back hair, and paunch.

Besides the rope and the knife, there was the Orchestra Hall ticket in Howe-Browne's name. The police had already determined that the seat he would have occupied was directly in front of John Harrison, still another NETT parent and a wealthy real-estate developer who once offered to "crush the life out of Corey" with some piece of heavy equipment, Crenshaw couldn't remember which.

And finally, there was the cassette tape in the Cadillac's player. The tape case was not found in the car or on Howe-Browne. The tape drew attention to itself and became a cue because it wasn't Howe-Browne's kind of music. It was James Brown music, *The Greatest Hits*. The next song up on the tape, near as they could figure, was "It's a Man's World," which came right after "I Feel Good."

But then it hit him—where was he, even with all

this evidence? Nowhere really, and yet everywhere. Ultimately the cues sent him back to the basics, to the truth that men get killed for four reasons: money, silence, a woman, revenge. The only one Crenshaw could safely eliminate was reason number three.

So now it was time to strike out in all directions. What he had, what somebody wanted him to think he had, was a conspiracy-of-fathers plot. Unfortunately, the dads he'd confronted didn't seem very nervous, didn't seem any more reluctant to shoot off their mouths now than they were at the trial. But their shouts and threats weren't very convincing, which may have been their purpose, Crenshaw realized, meaning their kids weren't the only good actors in the family. That thought sent Crenshaw after Tommy Doyle, Roger Doyle's victimized son, a fourteen-year-old who looked younger—a characteristic common to the boys involved with Howe-Browne. Maybe the kids know something, Crenshaw surmised. Maybe they know more than they think. Maybe they know a lot more than they're telling.

When Crenshaw decided to pay Tommy another visit, he wasn't worried about the right to have an attorney present. He just wanted to have a little heart to heart.

Crenshaw caught up to Tom Doyle between classes at the NETT complex. The detective knew Tommy wasn't due at his next session for over an hour. When he spotted the boy, Crenshaw walked up and said, "There's something you want to tell me. I just know it."

Young Doyle looked up at the detective, the same one who'd been at his house the other night, the one who'd gotten his father so upset. Tom shook his head and turned to leave.

"Well, we'll see," said Crenshaw pleasantly. "I'd like to ask you some routine questions. Nothing official, no big deal, okay?"

"My dad said not to."

"Not to what?"

"Talk to anybody about anything. Unless Mr. Kaplan is with me."

Crenshaw took a moment to reply. "Son, I know the rules. I know when it's worthwhile to have a lawyer holding your hand. But this isn't one of those times. It's only an inquiry at this point. Anything you say now is off the record. How's that sound?"

". . . I still can't. I shouldn't. My dad . . ."

Crenshaw knew he was getting somewhere. Here was a kid with a story, he'd bet anything. He'd seen the same look when he'd been in vice and juvenile justice. Kid wants to talk, share. "How about this?" Crenshaw continued. "You maybe don't want to say anything, but I do. How would it be if I said some things and you just listened, let me know if I'm hot or cold."

"Look, I gotta go now. I'll be late for class."

"Doesn't meet for an hour," said Crenshaw, glancing at his watch, then his notebook. He stared down at Tom Doyle. And slowly Tom wandered over to one of the benches lining the hall, sat down, and looked at the floor.

Crenshaw eased himself down quietly, careful not to change the mood.

"Here's the deal," he began. "The big thing right

now is still the rope, that Shur-Go stuff I was asking your dad about. I mean, I've looked and looked, run all over the place, and that Shur-Go just isn't very easy to find, you know?"

Still looking down, Tom gave a small nod.

"I called *everywhere*, and the only guys who buy it and use it are landscape guys, and only a few of them, specialists. Just your dad and three others, to be exact. You getting the drift here, Tom?"

Tom shook his head once.

Crenshaw whispered, "I figure maybe you're in the picture somewhere."

Tom looked up quickly, met Crenshaw's disturbing stare. "I thought you weren't accusing me!"

"I'm not. Don't get upset."

"I'm not upset." Tom turned away again, as though the move might make Crenshaw disappear.

Crenshaw watched the boy carefully, saw him purse his lips, clench his fists.

"All I'm saying is I'm pretty sure the rope came from your garage or some job site of your dad's. I don't know if you took it or who used it or anything. Maybe someone stole it from you, huh? Or borrowed it without telling you why . . ." Crenshaw let it hang, waited patiently, not moving a muscle, putting the pressure on Tom to end the embarrassing, incriminating silence.

"Wasn't my idea," he said at last.

"What wasn't?" Crenshaw asked.

"The rope. I didn't want to tie anybody up."

Oh, boy, thought Crenshaw, knowing he was somewhere now.

"Who did?" asked Crenshaw.

"Did what?"

"Made you tie him up?"

Tom waited a long time to answer. ". . . I can't talk to you anymore." He tried to stand. Crenshaw reached out smoothly and gently took hold of the boy's arm.

"My friend," he said in his deepest timbre, "we've got a homicide problem here. And I can't quit until it's cleaned up. And I don't want the wrong people bothered if I can find the right people, the ones who deserve the aggravation. You see where I am?" Man oh man, was he dancing.

Just then another boy, a delicate blond, came around the corner, stopping short, gaping at Crenshaw and Tom Doyle.

"Yeah, well," said Tom loudly. "I gotta go now. Sorry I couldn't help you." He jerked his arm free of Crenshaw's soft grip and headed toward the other boy. But before Tom could reach him, the other kid spun around and hurried away. Tom flashed Crenshaw a quick, anxious look and ran off, trying to catch up to his classmate.

That evening, when what remained of the troupe had assembled for rehearsal, Crenshaw showed up again. As he came in, he scanned the nearly empty theater. He noticed one kid slouched down in a seat halfway up the far section. The young man had his knees braced against the chair back in front of him. When he noticed Crenshaw staring, the guy pulled his head farther into his shoulders. Playing inconspicuous, thought Crenshaw, as he worked his way toward the stage, sitting down finally in the front row.

After the interim director called for the first break, Crenshaw was on his feet and up to the stage. He introduced himself to the director, Ward, and asked if he could interview some actors, said he needed two rooms, small. Then he asked the identity of the blond boy he'd seen in the hall that afternoon, the one who'd spooked Tom Doyle. He wanted to confront both of them.

"Lee Caine and Tom Doyle," called out Lawrence Ward. Crenshaw watched carefully, saw the two boys stiffen, then exchange a quick furtive glance. Tom Doyle came forward first.

"C'mon, Lee, move it!" hollered the director.

As Lee Caine approached Crenshaw, he said, "I don't have to talk to you." Then pointing to Tom Doyle, he added, "He's lying."

"About what?" asked Crenshaw, knowing already he had the edge he wanted.

"Everything," Caine answered, glaring at Tommy. "He always lies."

Tom Doyle returned the look, then dropped his gaze.

"We gotta talk, guys," said Crenshaw, a hand on each boy's shoulder. Caine shrugged out of Crenshaw's grasp. Tom Doyle remained passive. Maybe resigned, Crenshaw hoped.

"This way, Detective," said the director, leading

Crenshaw and the boys to a short corridor lined with small, soundproof compartments, practice rooms for actors, singers, and musicians. Warm-up rooms.

Crenshaw stopped at the first one, said to the director, "Would you please wait here with Lee?"

"Of course."

"Thanks. Be right back."

With that Crenshaw led Tom Doyle to the farthest room. Once inside, he pointed to the only chair and said, "Go ahead, sit. Relax." Tom sat as Crenshaw quietly closed the door.

"First of all, I don't think you killed him—Howe-Browne. Not alone." Crenshaw was trying to project high seriousness, let Tommy know the police felt anything was possible in this case, and no one was above suspicion.

"I didn't!"

"I believe you. But . . ."

"But what?"

"But I bet you know more than anyone thinks."

"About what?"

"The rope, the Shur-Go."

"I want my dad here."

"That's just what I had in mind."

"Huh?"

Crenshaw liked the surprised look on Tom's face. He continued, "That's precisely what we're going to do, include Dad."

"When?"

"As soon as we understand each other."

Crenshaw waited for Tom to comment, but he didn't.

"What I mean is," added Crenshaw, "if you're somehow involved directly, and you make me work hard to prove it—and I will prove it—I'll hold things against you *personally*, understand?"

Tom Doyle kept silent, refused even to look up and meet Crenshaw's cold, probing gaze.

"You see, it's pretty obvious someone's trying to get us after your dad and the other fathers. It's so obvious it's a little scary. Also way too neat. So I'm fairly sure you and your friend down the hall know something you're not telling. And maybe he's going to be a little more helpful about this than you are. And maybe he'll be the one who benefits from helping instead of hindering my investigation." Again Crenshaw paused, gave Tom some time to absorb the implications.

Then Crenshaw asked, "So what'll it be? Help or hinder?"

A tense silence formed as the question went unanswered. Crenshaw watched Tom begin to fidget, bounce his heels on the floor, squeeze his hands together subtly.

"Okay," said Crenshaw. "Had your chance. Stay here." Crenshaw was into the drama now. You could hardly pull off this kind of thing anymore, the creeps sometimes knowing the system and the strategies better than you. Thank God for the naive. So, on with the show—Crenshaw gripped the knob and turned it. He had just begun swinging the door open when Tom called out, "Wait!"

Crenshaw held his pose but turned his flat, dark eyes on Tommy Doyle, zeroing in on the moment of truth.

"I can help," Tom said quietly.

Crenshaw didn't reply. Instead his breath caught in his throat at this gift of luck.

"Okay?" Tom looked pleadingly at Crenshaw. "I'll help, okay?"

Fine, thought Crenshaw. Very, very fine.

"So let's call your dad, have him get hold of Mr. Kaplan."

"Do we have to?"

"I'm sure we do. That's what you've been asking for."

"He'll get really mad when he finds out."

"I guess I'd risk it if I were you. Things are a little more complicated now."

Tom finally looked at Crenshaw's face. "Why?" he asked.

"Because Mr. Howe-Browne didn't die alone. They dragged the area again where they found the car and hooked a bashed-up ice-fishing house. There was an old man inside."

After practice the same night, Angela said to Eddie, "Did you see that?"

"What?"

"That black cop's been around here a lot. He stops guys in the hall, pulls them out of class. He disrupts everything, even rehearsal."

"Has he talked to the Doyle kid before?"

"Uh-huh."

"Who else?"

"The guys like Tommy."

"Howe-Browne's kids," said Eddie.

"Yeah."

"What's he think, *they* did it?"

"How should I know? What a stupid thing to say."

"Just wondering. Don't get offended."

"I'm not offended . . . yet."

"What are you, then?"

"Excited," she answered, giving him a look.

chapter **8**

By late afternoon the next day, Crenshaw had worked out the terms of the immunity agreement with Roger Doyle, Tom Doyle, and Richard Kaplan. According to the *deal* (a seldom-used option for Crenshaw), Tommy would tell all he knew but would be neither charged with a crime nor forced to testify against any of his peers. Crenshaw was taking this gamble because he was convinced Tom Doyle knew enough to give them much more, maybe all of it. Crenshaw was instinctively sure by now Tommy was involved in something far more sinister than the boy realized, far more complex than he could imagine. The session with Tom and Kaplan was scheduled for 7:30 P.M.

* * *

Over lunch at a Burger King only four blocks from Nicollet High, Angela said to Eddie, "Guess what?"

Eddie said, "What?"

"My parents are going away this weekend."

"Really."

"And I'm house-sitting . . . alone."

"What are you, an only child?"

"Uh-huh. You, too, I suppose."

"I am," said Eddie. "They just leave you, huh?"

"Sure. Then I can do whatever I want. I mean, to hell with them, right?"

"That's great," Eddie replied. "Isn't it?"

"It's what they have to do."

"Why?"

"For not paying attention to me. I've got 'em on the ultimate guilt trip."

"They don't care?"

"Not really. Not anymore."

"They're paying for NETT," Eddie pointed out. "They care."

"Uh-uh," Angela insisted. "My father's trying to buy me off with the theater instead."

"Instead of what?"

"Caring about me, about us as a family."

"So NETT's your family." Eddie was playing along now, thinking the conversation was turning a little maudlin and melodramatic.

"It *was* my family," said Angela. "But like everything else, that's corrupt, too. He ruined everything."

"Who did? Howe-Browne?"

"Yes, *Howe-Browne*."

"So no more family."

Angela nodded silently, looked down for a second, thinking about Corey and all he'd promised, all she had lost.

"You know, Angela," Corey Howe-Browne had said right after her stunning audition at NETT, "it's okay to come here for the same reasons as other kids. That's a perfect place for us to start."

They were alone in his office. They were conducting the "character interview," the last step in the NETT admissions process. Corey was standing next to her, gently patting her shoulder. Then he sat down.

Angela, trying to sound as precocious as she appeared to be on stage, asked, "Why *do* kids come here?"

"To become somebody," Corey said. "Or more precisely, to become *a* somebody, a unique member of a family that's bigger than life."

"I don't get it," Angela said, dropping her pose.

"This is a place," Corey explained, "where you will have the opportunity to find yourself, to put together a self that you can live with, a self you can admire . . . and love. Most actors are doing this whether they'll admit it or not. They choose roles in order to try out identities, personalities. They're always looking for a combination of traits and qualities that will work for them, give them a few moments of happiness and wholeness."

Angela had nodded, tried to look thoughtful, as if she grasped at least part of what Corey was driving at.

Shy as she was offstage, she couldn't stop looking at him, his dark, dark eyes.

"I'll do my best, Angela," he concluded warmly, "to find roles that will help you understand your talent and love yourself."

"Thank you," she had whispered, mesmerized, her head swimming now with excitement, all the possibilities.

"I want you to find your strength here," he added. "I want to help you free up and shape your extraordinary potential. That's what a family should do, right? Bring out the best in all its members?"

She felt a surge of energy then that she knew would carry her to the very top. She had never before felt so important, so essential to herself or anybody else. Corey had done that for her. He had convinced her that she possessed the genius to change everything for herself, to control anything. Corey had made her feel intensely, crucially *alive*. And she'd loved him for that.

And unlike most of the adults in her life up to that point, Corey had come through for a while. During her only full-time year with him, he had spent more time with her than with any of the other actresses in the school. He'd pointed her out to her other coaches who then took her progress even more seriously. He'd given her the "star" credibility she needed and deserved without isolating her from her peers, or making her a threat or a cause for resentment within the troupe. With one exception, Michelle, who bitched about everybody, none of the others were jealous of her and the privileges her talent had generated.

But then, Corey . . .

Angela looked up, found Eddie watching her, smirking. She shivered.

"Where've you been?" he asked.

"You be my family," she said suddenly. She tried to smile.

"Huh?" said Eddie.

"*You* be my family, okay?"

"Sure," he said, feeling quite unsure of where Angela had been or was going.

"You mean it?" she pressed, reaching across the table and taking his hand. "Really?"

"At least for today."

"That's a start," she said, squeezing his hand.

With his free hand, Eddie picked up his Coke, took two swallows, and set it down slowly, buying a little time.

"I've been around the block," Angela said out of the blue. "You realize that?"

"And it's been fun?" replied Eddie. "Going around the block?" He was struggling to stay cool and find a rhythm in Angela's disjointed comments.

"Absolutely it's been fun," she answered. Then, batting her eyes and speaking in a little-girl whine, she added, "C'mon, mister. *You* take me around the block. Pleeease?"

By now Eddie was totally lost. He said, "What're you asking?"

"For a date, I thought. Boldly hinting."

"With me?"

"Who else?" she said, looking around the restaurant. "When?"

"How about Thursday?"

"Your house?"

"Eventually, I suppose. There's a big NETT cast party we can go to first."

Eddie nodded. "That could be interesting," he said.

"Sure," she replied encouragingly.

Eddie smiled back and said, "Okay, it's a date."

"The date," said Crenshaw, glancing at his digital watch for the information, then writing it down in his notebook. He looked across the coffee table at Richard Kaplan, whose face remained impassive, cold, observant. Tommy Doyle sat on the sofa next to Kaplan. He seemed to be staring at Crenshaw's shoes. Tommy's parents were not present.

"Are we ready?" asked Crenshaw.

"I guess so," answered Kaplan. "Tommy?"

". . . Okay."

"The rope, then," began Crenshaw. "Let's start with that. Why'd you take the Shur-Go?"

Tom didn't respond immediately, and Crenshaw began to wonder if he'd heard the question. But before Crenshaw had to repeat it, Tommy said, "He liked to play tie-up games."

"Howe-Browne."

"Uh-huh."

"There's a name for that," said Crenshaw.

Tom nodded absently and took a deep breath. "I know," he said.

"But this time you tied *him* up."

"Yeah."

"Really. And then what?"

"Nothing."

"Nothing?"

"I mean, after he was tied up, I left him there."

"Where?"

"I can't say."

"You don't know?"

Tom looked off, a little knob of muscle forming where his jaws met.

"You wanna take forever, son. I don't have forever," said Crenshaw.

Crenshaw's comment was met with silence.

He continued, "What I do have is a deal that could go sour very fast, we don't start progressing."

"Just a minute," said Kaplan.

"Objection?"

"Phrase your questions precisely and you may extract precise responses."

"Of course, Counselor," muttered Crenshaw. Then, "Okay, let's try it again. Where'd you get the rope you used to tie him up?"

"From my dad's truck."

"Your dad has all kinds of rope. Why that particular one?"

"It said to."

"What said?"

"The note."

Oh my, thought Crenshaw. "What note?" he asked. "Where'd you get it?"

"At school, NETT. In my locker."

"Who wrote it?"

"I don't know."

"Think . . ."

"I mean it! I don't know!" Tom was getting very anxious now. Crenshaw assumed he was edging too close to the truth.

"Where's this note?"

"I burned it, just like it said."

"Uh-huh. What else did it say?"

"Where to take the rope."

"And where was that?"

"I can't say for—"

"Tom, you *can* say and you *will* say, whatever I ask. Otherwise—"

"What are you, Detective," interrupted Kaplan, "a slow learner? Maintain a civil tone."

Crenshaw stared unblinking at the attorney for a three count, then continued, "Where?"

"Out in Minnetonka, a house."

"Whose?"

"I don't know. It wasn't all built yet."

Already Crenshaw knew the story was far too complicated to be extemporaneous lying. The boy was imaginative, but he couldn't possibly be so meticulously false. At least that's what Crenshaw concluded.

"The place was unfinished," said Crenshaw. "Under construction?"

"Yeah, like that."

"How'd you get there? You don't drive."

"Well . . . sometimes. My dad lets me drive the truck around the job site sometimes."

"You drove his truck?"

"No."

"What'd you drive?"

"I didn't. I got a ride."

"With who?"

"Kyle."

"Kyle . . ." Crenshaw was flipping through his notes, "Manders?" he asked, looking at the list of victims.

"Uh-huh," replied Tom, looking down.

"He's old enough to drive?"

"Sixteen."

"He doesn't look sixteen," said Crenshaw. "Just you two?"

"And Lee," said Tommy.

"What time did he pick you up?"

"Around nine."

"At night?"

"Uh-huh."

"Which night, exactly?" Crenshaw asked, writing continuously now.

"March fifteenth, the Ides."

Crenshaw regarded Tom skeptically. "Why'd you say that, 'the Ides'?"

"It's from *Julius Caesar*."

"I know."

"It was in—"

"The note," guessed Crenshaw.

"Yes."

"Out at the house," Crenshaw continued, "who was with you there?"

"I'm not completely sure."

Crenshaw came very close to losing his precious cool but chose instead to ask very civilly, "Why aren't you sure?"

"We were in costumes, masks."

"You rode out there in costumes?"

"Uh-huh."

"And then what?"

"At the house we met two other guys."

"In costumes."

"Yes."

"But you knew who they were."

"Mike Harrison and Richard Russo," said Tommy, completing the list of victims. With the exception of Shawn Singer, who Crenshaw *knew* was sixteen.

Crenshaw inhaled deeply, then sighed audibly. "So what have we got?" he asked rhetorically, looking over his notes. "The night of March fifteenth, you went out to this unfinished home in Minnetonka with Manders and Caine. And you were met by Harrison and Russo."

"Uh-huh."

"And you're all wearing costumes."

"Yes."

"What kind of costumes?"

"I was a hangman."

"A what?"

"We all wore black suits and hoods, like executioners."

"The note said to do that?"

"Uh-huh. We were all dressed the same."

"But not Shawn Singer."

"I didn't see him."

"Was Howe-Browne there before you?"

"No. He didn't come till about ten minutes later."

"You didn't get cold waiting?"

"There was a kerosene heater inside the house. It wasn't so bad."

"Weren't you scared?" asked Crenshaw.

"No."

"Why not? Why wouldn't you be? I mean, you're told to go way out to Minnetonka late on a winter night to meet a convicted sex offender—"

"I wasn't afraid of Corey," cut in Tommy Doyle with surprising boldness. He looked up at Crenshaw, met his gaze, and said, "It makes me mad."

"What makes you mad?"

"The newspapers and TV. How they made him look. Like a monster or something."

"But he wasn't," prompted Crenshaw, trying to sound neutral and objective but scrambling to understand.

"No," Tom answered. "I mean, not at first."

Kaplan cleared his throat but said nothing.

Tommy continued, "He was always there when I needed him, someone to talk to, like when I was afraid of doing a scene or messing up a line. Or when the others criticized me."

Crenshaw nodded, said, "I understand."

"I could call him anytime," said Tom, "and he would help make things better."

"Make what better?"

"Being alone there. My parents . . ."

Tommy sneaked a look at Kaplan.

"Tom's parents travel in the off-season, during the school year," explained Kaplan. "They attend a good many industry shows." Then Kaplan nodded at Tommy and said, "Go on."

Tommy said nothing.

Crenshaw pretended to scan his notes. Finally he said, "And what he did to you, what got Mr. Howe-Browne in trouble, that didn't scare you?" Crenshaw lifted his eyes and made Tommy look away.

"Sometimes," said Tom. "But he told us it was just his way, how he could show us he cared. It was his special way, you know?"

Tommy gave Crenshaw a pleading look.

"You know?" he asked again.

Begging for sympathy, thought Crenshaw.

"I don't know," answered Crenshaw. "What I think is, you feel like you have to defend him to save yourself. But what he did was wrong, Tom. Wicked and not your fault. And now you have to see that."

A short pause elapsed before Crenshaw pressed on.

He asked, "What did Howe-Browne say when he showed up?"

"He asked what was going on, if this was a surprise party for him or something."

"What'd you say?"

"Nothing. We weren't supposed to talk at all, so we just nodded. He said great, he needed some fun and excitement."

"How'd he know when to meet you?"

"I'm not sure. Right when he got there he said something like, 'Hi, boys, I got your call.' Like that. He was smiling."

"Tom," said Crenshaw gently, "what did you imagine you were part of out there?"

"A practical joke, I guess. The idea was to scare him pretty good. Like he did to us sometimes. Only some of the guys, like Richard and Mike, they wanted to really hurt him."

"He didn't get suspicious when you tied him up?"

"No. He let us do it because of what we'd done before."

By now Crenshaw was having an even harder time dealing with Tommy's matter-of-fact attitude toward Howe-Browne. What he felt like doing was getting up, closing his notebook, saying "good riddance," and letting the case slide onto someone else's desk.

Instead he asked, "So you tied him up. What next?"

"We blindfolded him and helped him into his car."

Crenshaw took it all down. "And then?"

"I left with Kyle and Lee. Our part was done."

"You leave anything in the car?" asked Crenshaw.

"Whose car?"

"Howe-Browne's."

"Like what?"

"*Anything*. Any objects or papers, anything at all."

"No."

"Who drove him to the lake?" Crenshaw asked suddenly, hoping to surprise Tommy.

"I don't know," he answered calmly.

The truth, thought Crenshaw.

"And you don't have any idea who organized the . . . joke?"

"No. Everybody thought the other guy did it, but no one would take credit."

Crenshaw fixed his stare on Tom Doyle, looked for a twitch, a facial tick, any sign that he was lying. What he saw was a flickering smile that was close to a grimace.

"What's funny?" Crenshaw asked.

Kaplan cleared his throat again, letting everyone know he was still there.

"Nothing really."

"Sure there is. C'mon, tell me."

"I was just thinking of something Corey used to say after we . . . you know, afterward." Tom looked up and found Crenshaw's dark eyes.

"What'd he say?" asked Crenshaw.

"He always said, 'Oh, Tom, I've been a bad boy again, a very bad, bad boy.' " Tommy now stared anxiously at Crenshaw, his eyebrows raised expectantly.

Crenshaw waited a few seconds before saying, "That's funny?"

"Well, yeah. Considering."

"Considering what?"

"What happened, what I guess we did to him. It could be my line for a change, right?"

"Hilarious," Crenshaw replied.

chapter 9

On Thursday, Angela didn't show up until third hour. Eddie found her waiting for him outside his fourth-period class.

"You won't believe what I heard," she began when Eddie came close to her. "Won't *believe* it."

"About what?"

"My former director."

"Yeah?"

"That black cop watched us rehearse again last night, and Tommy Doyle was missing."

"So? What'd he do, take off?"

"Took cover, I think. With the police."

"He was in on it?" Eddie asked in disbelief.

"Somehow."

"But *he* couldn't kill anybody. He's too small."

"He wasn't alone. That's what everybody thinks."

"Like who?"

"All of us."

"Uh-huh."

"The detective pulled Tom's best little buddy at NETT, Lee Caine."

"No friend of yours, I suppose."

"Lee's okay. But he was one of Corey's special favorites."

"Charming."

Angela rolled her eyes.

"So Tommy's a protected witness or something?"

"That's for openers." Angela glanced at her watch. "Look," she said, "there's a lot more to tell. Let's cut during lunch. Walk around Lake Harriet."

"Why not? Too nice to be here."

When fourth hour finally ended, Eddie was out of the room quickly. He went straight to the exit where Angela said she'd meet him, feeling more apprehensive with each step. The girl was different all right. He purposely shuffled the last steps toward the escape door, trying to look calm, detached. Only . . . Angela wasn't there to appreciate the attitude.

Eddie looked up and down the nearly empty hallways for her. He even peeked outside. No Angela anywhere. Then the last bell rang, leaving Eddie Limerick in no-man's-land. That's when he saw him coming, checking the corridors. For potential witnesses, thought Eddie. Because Alex James had his intimidating sights set on Clay Pigeon Limerick, sure as hell.

Finally Alex came face to face with Eddie.

"You all by your lonesome," Alex pointed out.

"I guess," said Eddie, struggling to effuse confidence and cool.

"You don't know what you're dealin' with," said Alex, shifting to a topic he hadn't revealed to Eddie.

"What are we talking about?"

"All you guys," Alex continued, his face tightening.

By now *Eddie* was looking for witnesses, the vice-principal, *anybody*.

"I don't follow," Eddie offered.

"She poison, man. You dumb or what?"

And that's when Eddie understood.

"Angela Favor," he said.

"Poison," said Alex. "Any guy she with."

"I thought you liked her. Willis said—"

"Willis maybe talk too much," blurted Alex. "Or you don't listen so good."

"You don't want to see her."

"See her *gone!*"

". . . Why?"

"Maybe you don't know she was there," said Alex, stepping even closer.

"Where?" asked Eddie, trying to back off.

"*There*, man. With my brother."

"The night he was . . ."

"Beat on," said Alex. "Clubbed."

"She never said—"

" 'Course she *never said*," Alex cut in, taking a final step toward Eddie, putting his huge hand on Eddie's chest. "There's a whole lot about that night she don't tell."

"Like what?"

"Like how she stood there and watched it happen. Stood there and let it happen." Then Alex really bore into Eddie with his terrifying stare. "Limerick, man, she *made* it happen."

Alex had filled his fist with Eddie's shirt and didn't even know it.

Before going to his last class, Eddie hunted down Willis and asked, "What's the deal about Alex's brother?"

"Why?" answered Willis.

"I'm curious."

"He talk about it? Alex?"

"I wouldn't say *talk*. More like threaten."

Willis smiled, said, "Ahhhh."

"So who is he?"

"Was. Not the same guy."

Eddie gave Willis a confused look, then asked, "Where is he now?"

"Transferred."

"But where?"

"Special school someplace."

"How bad was he hurt?"

"They call it a head trauma, you know? He look okay, but he ain't there. Gone simple."

"What was he like before?" asked Eddie.

"Adrian," said Willis thoughtfully. "Ol' Adrian, man, he was an *artist*. So graceful at everything. 'Course he played ball. All-City last year. A talent, you know? And the boy could paint. He never show his best stuff to anyone wasn't tight with him, but the work got *quality*, you know? Real, real pure."

"What about him and Angela?"

"She set him up, man."

"That's what Alex said."

"Well, Adrian, see, he wanted to try out acting, too, be a star. Girl said she could get him in the door, audition at some theater."

"The NETT."

"Uh-huh. So she help him train for it."

"What about the night he got hurt?"

Willis showed Eddie an odd smile. "She hurt him every night, man, doin' whatever."

Eddie let that sink in. "I don't understand," he said.

"'Fraid you will. Hey, gotta fly."

And before Eddie could respond, Willis had disappeared into the crowd.

chapter 10

After school, after being confronted by Alex James and enlightened by Willis, Eddie had lots of questions, most of them for Angela. But before he could call her from Aunt Cyn's, she phoned him.

She opened with, "Where'd you go?"

"Where were *you*?" countered Eddie. "I don't like being stood up."

"Well, don't start crying or anything."

"It was a helluva scene is what I'm saying."

"For me, too."

"Not like mine."

"Why not?"

" 'Cuz I was cornered by a guy who's really obsessed with you. And doesn't like me much either."

"Alex James."

"That's right."

"I think he's crazy. And dangerous," Angela declared.

"He says the same about you."

"I can imagine."

"I couldn't."

"Couldn't what?"

"Imagine you doing what he says you did."

Eddie anticipated the pause that followed.

"And what's that?" Angela finally said.

"Witnessing a beating, not stopping it."

There was another strained silence. "Do we have to talk about all that?"

"I think we better."

"Not on the phone."

Fifteen minutes later Eddie was walking, halfway to Angela's house, when he spotted her driving slowly toward him—in her mother's BMW. He stepped to the curb and watched her coast up and pull over.

"Hey, hi," she said, leaning toward him across the front seat. "Momsy went out with friends and forgot to hide her keys."

"Great," said Eddie without enthusiasm. He climbed in, pulled the door shut, hard. He stared at Angela, waited for her to say something.

"About what happened at lunch," she began, "I couldn't lie my way out of class early enough to meet you. We had a big unit test."

"What, it just slipped your mind?"

"Uh-huh."

"I don't believe you."

"I don't care."

"No, I guess you don't."

When Angela failed to reply, Eddie reached for the door handle. "See ya," he said, starting to get out.

"Oh, c'mon!" she said brightly, the bubbly flirt again. "Don't be so petty and prissy and self-righteous. I'm sorry, all right? I really did forget, about the test I mean."

"I don't want to hear you're sorry."

"What do you want to hear?"

"How about the truth?"

"The truth about what?"

"Anything. Any topic. Your choice, just to see if you can do it."

"You name something."

"Alex's brother."

"That's simple. I dated him a little. I guess he wanted to join NETT."

Eddie waited for more, but Angela had already stopped talking. "And that got him slammed?" Eddie asked to prompt her.

"I said it was simple."

"Who jumped him?"

"The guy I was seeing before Adrian."

"Keep going," said Eddie. "Where'd it happen? How?"

"We were coming out of this apartment building.

We'd been watching movies with a friend of Adrian's. Mark was waiting in the parking lot."

"Mark's the old boyfriend."

"Yeah, Mark Millerin. My *ex*."

"He was alone?"

"I thought so. But then I knew he wouldn't fight Adrian without some help."

"What'd he do, follow you around on dates?"

"He knew I'd be there."

"How come?"

"Because he kept calling, kept wanting to see me again. The guy wouldn't stop bothering me, you know? Just kept hanging around. So I told him about Adrian."

"And he caught you in the lot."

"Uh-huh. He called Adrian some names, told him to leave me alone. Adrian tried to be cool about it. We both knew Mark was drunk. I don't think he ever saw the billy club."

"Did you?"

"I knew Mark had one. He always talked about it. 'Genuine police issue,' is what he said. He brought it along in his car whenever he went downtown."

"Wound pretty tight, huh?"

"He hated black guys," Angela said calmly. "He was always afraid of getting mugged."

"Why'd he hate black guys?"

"How should I know?" she said irritably. "Why does anyone hate black guys?"

Eddie asked, "Did you really know Adrian?"

"Everyone knew Adrian. He was big-time at Nicollet."

"Big-time?" asked Eddie, not wanting to reveal all he'd learned from Willis. "At what?"

"You name it. Sports, music, painting, parties."

"So how many times did you guys go out before he got hurt?"

". . . Twice."

Eddie looked out the window, turned it all over in his mind. Then he asked, "Why'd you do it, really?"

"Why'd I do it?" she repeated. "What the hell are you driving at?"

"Why'd you go out with a black guy and then tell this Mark?"

"Simple," she said. "Everything's simple tonight. Pretty encouraging, huh?" She gave what he thought was a half-lidded come-on look.

"Why?"

"Because he took me for granted. He tried two-timing me and I didn't like it."

"So you got even?"

"It was his own fault. If he'd just paid attention, quit thinking about money . . ."

"Mark?"

"My goddam father! He—"

Angela stopped short, looked anxiously at Eddie.

"Your *father*?" he asked.

"Forget it, okay?" she said, staring straight ahead. "Look, could we just drop this?"

Eddie was confused. "He never hit you."

"Who, Mark?"

Eddie nodded. "That night," he said.

"He wanted to, I think. But then some people

jumped him and beat on him till the police came. Nearly killed him."

"Is he okay now?"

"He's around."

"Better off than Adrian?"

"I don't know."

Eddie listened without expression, watching for an opening, a way to see the logic of putting Adrian, Mark, and her father in the same scene. He couldn't believe she felt no responsibility for Adrian . . . or Mark. Finally he asked, "You feel bad about what happened?"

"Why should I?"

"You don't care about Adrian?"

"I don't feel much of anything for anyone sometimes. And Adrian . . . I hardly knew him, really."

Eddie wanted to get away from Angela for a while, think things through. But before he could leave she made him an offer she wouldn't let him refuse.

"Look," she began, "let's cheer up, start over."

Eddie glanced at her, then fastened his eyes on hers, searching for something.

"I mean," she continued, "I've got the car all night and some of the NETT guys are going to party. Remember?"

"So?"

"So you wanna come? It's a strange group, but sincere."

Eddie kept staring.

"C'mon," she persisted. "I'll even treat you to supper."

Eddie explored his options and saw nothing on the

horizon. And he still had questions for her. He replied, "I'm gonna call in first."

"Okay," Angela said. "Let's find a phone. Real fast."

At the party, which was held in a big top-floor apartment of a building near the NETT complex, Eddie did indeed meet a menagerie of personality types. Generally they all seemed pretty approachable even though each was trying awfully hard to seem original.

There was Saundra, a petite blonde in a purple body stocking, who greeted Eddie with a lopsided smile and a pat on the seat.

Before he could smile back, Angela was steering him toward Brian and Barb, the company couple, already enacting a remarkable public-display-of-affection scene. They stopped rubbing and grabbing each other long enough to shoot Eddie a quick, "Hi, guy."

Eddie felt another pull on his arm. When he turned he wasn't looking at Angela but at a yellow-haired boy about his size named Clinton, who said, "You're with Angela, right?"

Eddie nodded.

"This is my place, parents' place I mean. My dad owns the building and he keeps this apartment open for *private use*, understand?"

"Great," Eddie replied. "That's a good deal." He went back to scanning the room for Angela.

"She's in the john," Clinton explained.

"Oh."

"Can I get you anything, a drink?"

"That's okay," Eddie said. "I'm fine."

"So's she," said Clinton.

"Who?"

"Angela. She's the best we have, and she probably won't be with us very much longer. It's getting close to big break time for that girl."

"I suppose," Eddie replied.

"You haven't seen her work," said Clinton with a small frown.

"Not much, no. Just a rehearsal the other night."

"Well, she's a force, understand? So pay attention."

Just as Eddie was going to ask for a clarification from Clinton, he walked off and Angela came back. For the rest of the evening, Eddie listened to theater stories, jokes, and spontaneous bits of acting, scenes from previous productions. He left the party convinced this was a very bright crowd that respected and admired his date and wanted nothing to do with the memory of Corey Howe-Browne. The one time the ex-director's name was heard—Angela had mentioned him while reminiscing loudly about Eddie's violent audition at NETT—the reference generated a few laughs and no follow-up comments.

When Angela took Eddie back to Cyn's, she stopped just long enough for a quick kiss and a brief conversation.

"Have fun?" she asked.

"Uh-huh," he replied. "Something real different."

"They liked you," she said. "Especially that trampy Saundra."

Eddie looked over and found Angela smiling.

He arched an eyebrow. "You know anything more about her?" he asked. "Like her number?"

Instead of a standard courtesy chuckle, Angela gave Eddie a whimsical, far-off look. "I've got *your* number," she said. "You know that?"

chapter 11

You know anything about this, Mr. Wiseguy?"

Eddie was taken aback. Angela had been waiting for him the next morning just down from Goldman's door. She'd confronted him so aggressively he was stunned. She held up a piece of paper folded in half. He slid out of the surging hallway traffic and moved in close.

"What's that?" he asked.

"Oh, c'mon," she said. "You know exactly what it is. Nice work, Mr. *Limerick.*"

Eddie shook his head. "I'm lost," he replied, trying a puzzled look.

"You didn't write these, stick 'em in my notebook?" She waved the sheet at Eddie again.

Before Eddie could deny the accusation a second

time, she added, "Please don't play dumb now. You're a lousy actor, and lousy actors waste valuable time."

"That's because I'm not acting. Let me see."

She handed him the paper and he scanned it. There were four verses, limericks, all numbered like stanzas of a hymn, each neatly typed. And they were all about the same subject, Mr. Corey Howe-Browne. Eddie read them in sequence:

I

Who knows when sweet Corey first sought it,
Or whether he struggled and fought it.
If he did, then he lost,
Now we all know it cost
Him his job and his life, for he "bought" it.

II

To call the man's dive accidental,
And his loss to the world detrimental,
Is to turn a blind eye,
For we all know the guy
Was a *sicko* and so unessential.

III

Now the cops think they smell a gang hit.
So they shuffle the clues till they fit
Some Conspiracy Grand,
That should reach to the hand
Of the one with the guts for the bit.

IV

So who could have pulled it together?
Who studied the lake and the weather?

Who mastered the plan
That did in the man
Who liked to play love scenes in leather?

When Eddie was finished, he looked up and met Angela's probing stare.

"Well?" she said.

"What exactly is this?"

"Yours . . . exactly."

"Uh-uh. Wrongo. Never saw it before. Not me you should be chasing." He handed back the sheet.

Angela appeared instantly confused, fearful. He'd never seen her so upset, looking so perplexed.

"I'll call you after school," he offered. "We can talk about it then. Right now *I* gotta hurry. Just can't be late."

Angela glanced at him, nodded absently, said nothing, turned away, and wandered off.

"Could be someone from the theater, right?"

After school, Eddie had barely let himself into Aunt Cyn's duplex before calling Angela.

Now he cradled the phone between his chin and shoulder, his hands working open a note from the ACE.

"You take your books there sometimes," he went on. "I've seen you. Anyone could've planted it."

"Maybe. I don't know," Angela said. "Everything's so messed up now."

"Yeah, well, what's new. That's life, right?"

"I mean, whoever did this is trying to get *me* involved in Corey's death. I'm scared, Eddie."

"Probably just a joke."

"A pretty sick one."

"But skillful. Good limericks, speaking as an expert."

Eddie was trying to cheer her up, but he didn't hear any laughter. Finally, he asked, "Why's this bother you so much?"

"I just told you. Someone's trying to pull me into something ugly and terrible, and I don't like it."

"For no reason."

"Of course not."

"Well, don't let on you found the paper. At rehearsal keep your eyes open, see who's watching you."

"Oh, is that what I should do, Mr. Undercover Man?"

"Just trying to help."

"You could help by confessing."

"No can do."

"You'll be sorry."

"But innocent."

"Nobody's innocent who gets involved in this thing."

"You're right," Eddie said.

Angela took a deep breath. "Eddie?"

"Huh?"

"I'm glad you called. I really need somebody to talk to, a friend."

"Someone who has time for you."

"Uh-huh."

"Speaking of which . . ."

"What?"

"It's about the weekend."

"What about it?"

"I'm sitting here," said Eddie, "looking at my freedom papers."

"I don't understand."

"My dear aunt left me a letter saying she'll be in Rochester for the weekend, *allllll* weekend. 'Helping a friend,' it says."

"What a wonderful coincidence," Angela said brightly.

"Your parents are definitely gone?"

"To some resort near Brainerd. My father's country-club buddy owns it. He's throwing a big summer kickoff party."

"So what should we do under the circumstances?"

"That's up to you," Angela replied.

"When?"

"Anytime."

"I'll be over."

"Walk right in," she said.

Then she hung up without saying good-bye.

chapter 12

After dark, Eddie had wasted no time getting over to Angela's. But he did take his time entering the house. He felt just ambivalent enough about Angela to move in cautiously, scout the place.

So for half an hour, from across the street, down the block, then in the alley, Eddie watched the mansion, the few lighted windows, trying to determine if Angela was indeed home alone. When he finally convinced himself that luck and truth were real tonight, he circled the building again and approached the front door.

He knocked gently, but Angela didn't respond. He tried the knob, and the heavy door swung open into the dimly lit vestibule. Eddie slipped in and quietly closed and locked the door. He wanted to call out but then thought it best not to. His surveillance had assured him that the only upstairs light was coming from Angela's room, so he decided to go there directly rather than risk a search of the house. He headed for the staircase and began his ascent.

On the second floor he could see a thin bar of light spilling out of Angela's suite. He walked quietly and carefully down the long, dark corridor, his eyes set on Angela's door. He stopped outside and listened. All he could hear was Angela's TV. Eddie nudged the door open and found her sitting on a small couch, watching a videotape of herself in a past performance.

She turned her head slowly, sensing his presence. She smiled and offered him a languid, "Oh, hi." Then, "Come here and sit with me."

Eddie eased the door shut and crossed the room, joining her on the love seat. She took his hand and began stroking it, making little circles with her index finger.

"I thought you stood *me* up," she confessed.

Her breath was alcohol sweet and seductive, not at all unpleasant to Eddie.

"Never," he replied.

"You better not," she said, "you know what's good for you." Then she asked, "Want a drink, help you relax?"

"I'm relaxed," Eddie claimed, breathing shallowly already.

"C'mon," she insisted. "It's not good to drink alone."

She closed her eyes, tilted her head back. Then she moved away from him to pick up the wineglass she'd left on the end table.

"Maybe later," Eddie said. He turned his attention to the TV tape, feeling uneasy again.

"That's me in *Pinocchio*," she pointed out before taking a long pull from her drink.

Eddie kept watching, entranced.

Angela continued, "It was the last part I played when Corey still believed in me and I still trusted him . . . the bastard."

Eddie considered that comment before saying, "Why'd it end with *Pinocchio*?"

Angela said, "Maybe you're not as smart as I think."

"C'mon," said Eddie, facing her now.

"I mean it."

"His arrest," Eddie surmised. "That's when you knew you couldn't trust him, he was a liar, too."

"Long before that," Angela replied. She turned her attention to the tape and together they watched as the play ended and the crushing applause began.

"You're really good," commented Eddie.

She got up with her glass and walked over to the minifridge.

"What do you want?" she asked, opening the door, scanning the contents.

"Your parents let you drink?" asked Eddie.

"They know I'll do it anyway, so they ignore this." She was pointing to her stash of beer, wine coolers, and mix. "My father's not consistent, though. Sometimes he raids the thing and dumps what he doesn't approve of."

"I suppose."

"So, what'll it be?" she asked again.

"Whatever you're having," Eddie said, watching her take another glass from somewhere behind the refrigerator, pick up a half-full wine cooler, and pour it out for him. She then opened another bottle, refilled her glass, and moved gracefully back to the couch.

She handed him the drink and said, "Well, here we are, alone at last."

They touched glasses and Eddie took a sip. The drink was sweet and relaxing. He wanted to ask the flavor but feared showing his ignorance. He drank some more.

Angela took another big swallow, set down her glass with extreme care, and nuzzled close to Eddie, holding tight to his arm.

"Hey, kick off your shoes," she said dreamily. "Get comfortable."

She moved back to let him unlace his sneakers and push them aside. When he was done, she used her leg to pull a small hassock in front of them, and again she slid close. They put up their feet and cuddled.

"So talk to me," she murmured, her eyes closed.

Eddie was speechless, stunned, way out of his element all of a sudden.

"You wanna listen to some music or something?" he asked to break the silence.

"I'd rather listen to you. You tell me anything you want. Tell me about getting kicked out of basketball at Parker."

"Why?"

"You promised."

"I did?"

"You said it was a story, and I love a good story."

Eddie said, "You're pretty desperate."

"Just do it, okay?" Angela replied. "I want to hear you talk."

"Tell you how I got kicked out of basketball."

"Yeah, exactly."

"Lotta stuff."

"Like?"

"Like once I stayed in the locker room after the half-time speech to take a bath. We were playing at Moorland. They had this great Jacuzzi."

"And you got caught?"

"But not till late in the fourth quarter. I was so deep on the charts by then Coach didn't even miss me."

Angela laughed for the first time since Eddie's arrival. "And that did it?"

"Only the start. Lots more."

"I thought so."

"What finally got me canned was betting another scrub the coach wouldn't play me in our first region game, even if we got ahead by thirty. We were at Blue Hills Prep, buncha real saps."

"But rich, very rich."

"Uh-huh. Like I was gonna be. This other guy put up twenty bucks I'd see action. Then he talked four other players into betting for the coach and against me. I stood to win nearly a hundred fifty dollars."

"Or lose it."

"Exactly. See, I just couldn't lose. I couldn't afford it. I mean economically. So to make sure I'd *never* get in the game, I didn't wear anything under my warm-up pants. Then even if Coach *did* call my number, I couldn't possibly set foot on the court."

"Let me guess. The coach called—"

"Of course," Eddie said. "And when he did, and I got up to tell him my problem—like geez, I *forgot* my trunks—this other benchy yanks down my warm-up pants, trying to hurry me, win the bet."

"He didn't realize you weren't . . . you know, fully equipped?" Angela took her head off Eddie's shoulder and looked him in the eye.

He grinned.

"This is crazy!" said Angela, laughing again, falling back against the love seat. "Absolutely."

"Yeah. And my last move."

"They had to dump you."

"They had to," Eddie confirmed.

"You miss it?" she asked, suddenly serious.

"Sometimes. I was pretty good, really. I mean I *love* the game. But I don't like myself playing organized ball."

"On a team, at a school."

"Yeah, like that."

"You're not a team player."

"I don't think so, not at all."

"Then you're a nonconformist," she said with more excitement, seeming to have found compensation.

"I've been called that."

"And a rebel."

"That, too." Eddie laughed a little self-consciously.

"You're not *theirs*."

"Never."

"You're mine," she said, hugging Eddie again.

By now Eddie wanted to escalate, start kissing her and see where that would take him. But before he could make his move she asked, "You ever been in *real* trouble? With the law, I mean?"

"I know what you mean," he said. "Will you like me better if I have?"

She shrugged. "Have you?" she asked.

Eddie reached for his drink, his throat dry from talking, from anticipation.

"Have you?" she repeated.

"Technically," he answered. "Had some accidents."

"Car accidents?"

"One of 'em." Eddie laughed, remembering. "I was going to pick up a buddy," he began. "He was working at an Amoco station in Golden Valley. So I'm driving his car, this old beater Ford, and when I came flying into the station, going a little fast just to be funny, I hit the brakes and nothing happens, nobody home down there. Before I could stop I sheared off all three pumps on one island."

"No!"

"It was in the papers."

"What happened?"

"This *pal* never told me he wanted the car to work on the brakes."

She laughed. "I meant what happened to you? You get out of it?"

"I ran away."

"You fled the scene."

"Immediately."

"And they never caught you? Your friend didn't turn you in?"

"Naw. We were tight and he hated the station owner anyway. I guess he said the car just rolled across the lot by itself. There weren't any witnesses. It was real late."

"Clean getaway."

"Right."

"It's a great feeling, I suppose."

"What? Wrecking the pumps?"

"Getting away clean."

"I guess so, sure."

Angela snuggled in again, then gave him a passionate kiss. She pulled back, leaving him breathless. She said, "I like you. You're going to work out fine."

Eddie wanted her to explain, but before he could ask, Angela bolted up and shrieked, "My God!" Then she shoved Eddie away hard and cocked her head, listening.

"What?" he said.

"Shhhh," she said, covering his mouth with her hand. "They're home!" she whispered frantically. "They're *home!*"

Eddie's eyes went wide.

Finally he stammered, "But . . . but you said—"

"I know what I *said*," snapped Angela. "It's what they did. Came back early or something. Quick!" she said, pushing at Eddie again. "You've got to hide."

"W-where?"

"Under the bed. Someplace!"

"Don't be . . . be ridiculous," Eddie struggled.

"They're coming up to check on me right *now*. I can hear."

"I can't."

Then suddenly he did. The squeak of the hallway floor maybe, and Eddie became a believer. He pushed himself off the couch and searched for his shoes. He found just one. Before he could spot the other, Angela rasped, "Hurry, get in *there*. Hurry!"

With Angela shoving him along, Eddie stumbled toward the huge walk-in closet, which was predictably stuffed with dresses and blouses and sweaters and slacks and coats. He fell to his knees and burrowed between the garments and buried himself in the back. Angela closed the door behind him.

For a while Eddie tried to listen to the conversation among father, mother, and daughter, but the voices were muffled, the talk subdued. He had no idea what time it was. He decided the smart thing was to lay low, be quiet, and wait until he was sure everybody was gone, asleep. Then he could sneak off unnoticed.

So he sat there, cramped and suddenly dog tired, but safe. At least for the moment. As the close, fragrant, warm air, his own nervous exhaustion, and the wine conspired against him, he couldn't help thinking Angela was playing with him and getting a little too careless. It wasn't much longer before the effort of thinking, of analysis, seemed useless. So Eddie gave up and let go, let himself drift and slide and fall into a troubled sleep.

When Eddie woke up, the house was very, very quiet. He had to think a moment to remember where he was and how he'd gotten there. After listening to the stillness for another minute, Eddie decided to venture forth. He silently crawled out from under the piles of designer clothes that had hidden him. He cautiously stood up in the closet, made sure he had his balance. Then he slowly pushed open the closet door.

Angela's room was dark. Eddie stood in the blackness, trying to recall if any lights had been on when he'd taken cover, so long ago. He had no idea if it was still Friday night or Saturday morning. What a mess, he thought. He should've followed his instincts and passed on this one.

He walked carefully to the nearest window and peeked behind the shade. It was night, very late, no traffic moving. Eddie wanted to get the hell out fast but he still hadn't found his other shoe. He felt around for it on the floor of the pitch-black room and had no luck. He knew that to find it and make his escape he had to risk turning on a light.

He remembered where her desk was, which corner of it held the small high-intensity reading lamp. He located the switch and flicked it on. He glanced over at the bed and found it empty, still neatly made.

Looking down, he spotted the lost shoe at his feet. He'd apparently kicked it across the room, where it had knocked over a wastebasket, spilling the contents. He bent to retrieve the shoe and right the basket.

While replacing the crumpled papers in the little wicker basket, he discovered three or four half-torn sheets with verses, Angela's poetry, about him or them maybe. Eddie carefully pieced one of the sheets together. He wanted to read her thoughts, share her secrets. It took him only a few lines to see what he had—rough and final drafts of the limericks she'd tried to credit him with writing. His heart slowed and beat painfully.

Still holding the sheets, he glanced at the old electric typewriter on the other end of the desk. He leaned closer, picked it up, and inspected it carefully, top and bottom. He set it down and slipped one of the limerick fragments into the machine and retyped a line. The print was the same. Then he took a pencil and wrote down all of the brand and model information listed on the machine. He pocketed the evidence, shut off the desk lamp, and tiptoed out of Angela's room.

As he stood in the dim hallway, listening again for any sign of activity, company, trouble, Eddie found himself stunned. He'd been suddenly shocked by the possibility that the limericks might be accurate, even prophetic. What if that black cop was hassling the guys at NETT because the police actually believed in a conspiracy theory? How much did Angela really know about the crime? How much was just grandstanding on her part?

While mulling over these notions, Eddie also found himself looking through the half-opened door of the bedroom next to Angela's. It was obviously more than a guest room. On the door was a little tarnished brass sign he'd never noticed before—KEV'S APT.

Eddie moved slowly into the room, noiselessly shut the door. He felt for the light switch, found it, held his breath, and snapped it on. What he saw confused him even more.

He was in a boy's bedroom, the former digs of Kevin Favor, quite an athlete and scholar if the football and golf trophies and many framed certificates of merit were any indication. On the desk across the room sat a five-by-seven family picture bordered in antique brass. It showed all four of them on a yacht, sipping fruit drinks in the cockpit of a huge motor sailer.

Eddie took in the rest of the place with one final sweep, then backed off. Soon he was into the hallway, down the stairs, and out of the house.

All the while he was walking home he kept asking himself, Why'd she lie about having a brother?

Had she lied about everything?

chapter 13

Very early Monday morning, Crenshaw clapped his hands, let out a yelp that echoed through the empty squad room. He'd done it. At last he'd gotten what he wanted. You always get it, he thought, if you're patient and relentless and smart. You had to be smart, know exactly who to play, and when and how.

He'd been all those things, but he'd never seen a sweeter payback for his diligence. He'd found his opening, explored its defenses, discovered the ultimate weak spot. And it wasn't Tommy Doyle. In this venture, Tommy had been a *good* soldier. He'd followed his orders to the letter. When isolated and confronted, he'd caved in quickly, but during the operation itself he hadn't hedged his bets. Never saw a reason to, probably.

But not everyone followed orders to the letter. Or more accurately, orders in the letter and about the letter. Crenshaw had sensed it even at their first meeting, and now the accuracy of his intuition was confirmed, again. Lee Caine was as self-devoted as Crenshaw suspected. And he was the one who had broken rank and given Crenshaw his edge.

Caine had not only kept and hidden the crucial itinerary letter; he'd also nearly begged Crenshaw to accept it, take it off his hands and mind. Lee was obviously hoping it would give him an edge in the race to turn state's evidence and avoid implication or even prosecution. Only Lee Caine didn't know Tommy Doyle had already crossed the finish line.

Still, there it was, right in Crenshaw's hand, the mystery letter—the blueprint of a murder. Lee Caine's part in a murder, anyway. No, a *double* homicide. They mustn't forget Emile Kozlicki, even though everyone else apparently did. Crenshaw had never seen anything like that either.

When Kozlicki died with Howe-Browne, *no one* missed the old man. No one reported his disappearance or voiced any concern. He seemed to have no relatives. The only information Crenshaw had gathered came from another retiree whose shack was closest to Kozlicki's. He'd said, "Ol' Emile's usually the last one off the ice each spring. Loves his fishin', you know? Guy takes fines every year for stayin' out past the deadline."

And thinking of deadlines, mused Crenshaw as he read through Lee Caine's letter again, he reminded himself to make some copies of it immediately, then send the original to the lab. He knew those boys could quickly give him the specifics, a name for the typeface, maybe even the make of the machine that typed it.

Late Monday afternoon, Eddie lay on his bed at Aunt Cyn's. The shades were down, the room was dark, and he was thinking. He wondered how he'd gotten caught up in something so *strange*. He was trying to look at it from all sides, see if he could figure out exactly what the hell Angela was doing, and why.

If she'd actually written the limericks (and it seemed certain she had), what was she trying to prove? Was it all just an act, another face, a little look-at-me routine? Or could she know a lot more than she was telling about the whole Howe-Browne case? Did he want to know what she knew? Did he even want to see her again? He had to face the truth now: She scared the hell out of him.

That morning, for example, he'd pretended to leave for school but had doubled back as soon as ACE left the apartment to attend an "assignment meeting" at some magazine editor's office. Then he placed himself right where he was now. During the long hours of escape and contemplation, phone calls had come and gone unanswered. In the silences between calls Eddie let his imagination roam far and wide.

As the afternoon wore on, he wore out and finally drifted off to sleep. He didn't wake up till he heard:

"Eddie, is anything wrong?"

"Huh?" he said, suddenly alert, anxious.

"It's just me," replied Cyn.

Eddie looked toward the light and saw her silhou-etted in the doorway. He asked, "What time is it?"

"Nearly time for supper."

"Oh."

"You sure you're all right?"

"Uh-huh."

"Tired? Busy day at the factory?"

"Yeah."

Cynthia paused before turning to leave. As she did she said to Eddie, "The news just started, and they're going to interview some cop who's been working on the Howe-Browne thing, in case you're interested."

"Today's installment," said Eddie.

"The drama builds."

Eddie gave her a weak laugh. "There's no business like show business," he said.

"There's no business *but* show business. C'mon."

Eddie asked, "What's for supper?"

"Chef's surprise."

"Uh-oh," he said, getting up.

"You don't trust me?"

"At Nicollet that means *danger*, chef's surprise. Visions of mystery meat and silt gravy."

"O ye of little faith," Cyn replied.

She finally left to check the progress of their meal while Eddie stood and stretched. Then he shuffled into the front room, sat down on the couch, and watched the news.

He hadn't been staring more than a few moments before he saw him again, filling up the screen with his intimidating bulk, the detective who'd been haunting the NETT's rehearsals for most of the week.

Crenshaw was saying that finally the investigation was "taking focus."

"And what does that mean?" asked the reporter.

"It means evidence is emerging with multiple implications."

The reporter smiled. So did Crenshaw. The attractive, well-dressed woman continued, "Have you answered my question, Detective?"

"Generally."

"At least that. But can you be more specific?"

"Not without blowing the case."

"But you're ready to call it a murder, unequivocally?"

"You bet."

"And you have suspects."

"Several."

"Is there a front-runner?"

"They run as a pack, at this point."

The reporter looked momentarily confused, then brightened and said, "A conspiracy?"

"No comment," answered Crenshaw.

"Could you describe the evidence, generally?"

"Documents, generally. Typed." Then with a theatrical flare, Crenshaw brought up his forearm, glanced at his watch, and said, "Look, I've gotta get back to work, okay?"

"Of course, Detective. Thanks for your time, and good luck."

Crenshaw nodded at the reporter, smiled into the camera, and stepped out of the picture.

Eddie, openmouthed, slowly expelling his breath, heard nothing after Crenshaw's departure. The only words in his mind were "documents typed."

"What's the matter?" asked Cynthia.

Eddie snapped out of it. "What?" he said.

"I'm wondering, where's the ghost?"

"Getting spooky, that's for sure," he answered.

"What now? I missed it."

"The detective, Crenshaw, he says they've found evidence that Howe-Browne's death was a murder and maybe a group project."

Cyn narrowed her eyes, tried to look skeptical. "You mean the parents?"

"He didn't say."

"It could be done, I suppose. And dispersed guilt might not be shared guilt, at least for the guilty."

Eddie nodded absently.

After supper, as Eddie helped Cyn clean the dishes, she said, "You certainly seem distracted."

"Yeah?" Eddie replied, trying to move easy, sound relaxed.

"You hardly ate. You aren't being the wise guy. What's up?"

"Mondays at Nicollet, they do that, take the edge off."

"I imagine."

Eddie worked in silence for a few minutes more.

Then he put down the towel and said, "I'm going for a walk."

"Want some company?"

"I need to be alone, do some thinking."

Cynthia smiled. "Anytime you want to talk . . ."

"I know. Thanks."

Eddie left the house and headed toward the park. More than anything now he needed to be moving, going somewhere. He knew what he wanted to do: He wanted to call that detective and run a few things by him. It seemed to Eddie that somehow everything was connected to everybody in this Howe-Browne thing, and if he grabbed hold of enough threads he might work his way up to . . . what? The one hand pulling *all* the strings?

There were lots of people who wanted the ex-director dead, gone forever. But like the limerick Angela had shown him suggested, some one person must have organized it. Wouldn't that be logical?

As Eddie passed the 7-Eleven and spotted a pay phone, he decided to call Crenshaw. It took several reroutings by the precinct operator and a few minutes on hold before Eddie heard Crenshaw's by now familiar voice say, "This is Crenshaw."

"I saw you on TV," Eddie began awkwardly.

"Great. Who's this?"

"You said you found some evidence that was typed."

"Right."

"What I want to know," continued Eddie, not giving Crenshaw another chance to ask his name, "what I'm wondering is, could the stuff have been typed on a . . ." he pulled the slip from his wallet and read, "a Smith-Corona Coronet Super 12?"

Eddie waited for Crenshaw's reply, but the detective hesitated, paused just long enough to let Eddie know he had something.

Finally Crenshaw asked, "Who am I talking to, please?"

Eddie didn't respond. Instead he hung up and walked quickly away from the phone, from the lights of the convenience store. He started running as he entered a dark side street that he followed for five or six blocks. Then he thought, They can trace calls real fast nowadays, even to pay phones. He thought, My fingerprints are all over that receiver.

At the next busy intersection he stopped, wondered where he was running to, what exactly he was running from. Unable to answer his doubts, he resolved to keep looking, to learn more, to learn enough to see the whole truth, as if that were possible. As a precaution, though, he doubled back to the pay phone to wipe off his prints. When he saw an elderly woman in the booth gripping the receiver with both hands, Eddie smiled to himself and headed home.

Eventually he wandered into Aunt Cyn's. She greeted him with, "You had a call when you were out."

"Yeah? Who?"

"Why, your sweetie, your little guardian Angela."

chapter 14

On Tuesday Eddie managed to get into school and Goldman's class without seeing Angela. He knew she'd catch up to him sooner or later, but he wanted to delay the confrontation as long as possible. By noon, Eddie had concluded that Angela wanted what he wanted. She wasn't in school at all.

It was when Eddie's guard was down, almost completely, that Angela appeared. He was walking home, his mind pleasantly blank, at the precise moment Angela pulled alongside the curb and called out to him, saying, "I suppose you want an explanation."

Eddie stopped, shivered, then tried to play it slow. He gave her a casual look, shuffled to the car, and leaned down to look in.

"I see how things are," he said.

"You do?" Angela replied, showing a little smile. "You talk to my parents or something?"

"Huh?"

"About why I left you stranded Friday night, why I've been up north since then. I don't blame you for being mad."

"No, I meant . . ."

"What?"

"Howe-Browne."

"You see Howe-Browne?"

"You're involved, right?"

She gave him a strange, quirky grin. "C'mon," she said. "Get in. There's so much to tell."

"Where're we going?"

"Where else? My place."

"I don't think so."

"Nobody's home."

"That's what scares me."

"No surprise visitors, okay?"

"That's what you said—"

"*Last time*," Angel cut in, stealing Eddie's line.

"Uh-huh."

"Trust me," she said warmly. "C'mon, get in."

So Eddie climbed in, mesmerized by this strange, beautiful girl.

"Why'd you go up north?" asked Eddie.

"Momsy talked my father into taking me along, thought we needed a little togetherness. Their counselor must have called them on the car phone or something. I mean, they were halfway to Brainerd before they decided to include me. So when they came back and you took cover, we all had a "family" discussion for about ten hours. Which means Daddy talked, Momsy nodded, and I faked consciousness. Then we all piled in the car and left for the resort. It was pretty late. What'd you do, fall asleep?"

"Uh-huh," Eddie said, remembering he'd gotten home at about three o'clock that night.

"You found your way out."

"Yeah."

"Well, up north was real dead."

Eddie waited for more.

But Angela began humming, and the conversation lapsed completely until she pulled into her long, curving driveway.

When they were at last behind the closed door of Angela's bedroom, Eddie scanned the area, asked, "Where's your typewriter?"

"What typewriter? What're you talking about, typewriter."

"The one that was there," Eddie said, pointing. "I saw it last time."

Angela gave him a knowing smile, the sly grin of the inside joker. "Eddie, it's the computer age, word processing. Nobody has typewriters anymore."

Eddie stared back at her, tried to chew his gum deliberately, look cool and detached while he bought time to draw conclusions.

"Why're you so interested in typewriters?" she asked, her voice self-consciously coy.

Eddie waited a moment more, then asked, "Just exactly what the hell is going on?"

"Nothing yet," answered Angela.

Eddie put on the cold stare. "What're you trying to prove?" he asked. "Why are you playing games with this?"

"This what?"

"All this," Eddie said, sweeping his arm to include the whole room—the bed, the closet, the bulletin boards filled with theater clippings. "I mean you've lied to me so much it could take a week to straighten everything out."

"Lied how?" she responded. "When?"

"You said you were an only child. You aren't."

"So?"

"So you lied."

"So maybe you don't understand. I *am* an only child, an all-alone-only child. The only thing Daddy does to acknowledge my presence is sign checks for NETT."

Eddie offered a questioning, encouraging look but she didn't notice. "So where's Kevin?" Eddie asked.

"Dead," Angela replied, looking at the floor.

"Is that the truth?"

Glaring at Eddie she snapped, "Yes, that's the truth!"

"When did he die? How?"

"In a scuba-diving accident almost two years ago in Florida. We were out together exploring a coral reef. He tried to scare something out of a crevice and got hung up. I went for help, but nobody could get to him fast enough. He panicked and tore his air hose on the coral. My father thinks it was all my fault."

"He said that?"

"He'd never be so direct and honest. But it's how he feels. I know it."

"Was it your fault?" asked Eddie.

She fixed on him again, her eyes unblinking. "You don't believe me either," she said.

"What do you care?"

"You're making me a liar, too. Just like Daddy."

"You're lying about the typewriter," Eddie continued.

"Am I?"

"I *saw* it," he repeated, "along with all the limericks." Eddie waited for her to be surprised, even shocked and embarrassed at being found out, but he needn't have.

"I like that," she said coolly. "You notice things."

"Why'd you do it?"

"What?"

"Why'd you let me find them? You want to get caught, right? You wanted me to catch you." Eddie wasn't ready yet to tell her he'd saved two of the drafts.

"I don't want to be *caught*," Angela replied. "I want to be *recognized* and *appreciated*." She seemed to be waiting for Eddie to say something, see the big picture.

"You lost me," he said.

"C'mon, Eddie," she continued, her voice changed, low and purring now. "Let's relax a little, huh? Can't I make you feel good?"

"You make me nervous."

"Forget it, then. Who needs you, any of you?" Her voice was suddenly hard and sharp.

"*Any of you?*" he repeated.

She tried an amused look. "Maybe I spoke too soon. Maybe you're like all the rest. Maybe you *can't* get it."

"What're we talking about now?" Eddie stared back at her and saw the ironic smile still on her face, annoying because it seemed to be mocking him.

"I better go," he said. "This is getting too strange."

"You're so *stupid*," she said pleasantly.

"You want accusations?"

"I dare you."

"You set up Howe-Browne."

"Oh really."

"Somehow you got other people to do it, kill him, while you stood by watching."

"And where'd you get that idea?"

"From the cops, who I'm pretty sure have some evidence typed on your typewriter, the one you've conveniently never owned all of a sudden."

"I never owned a typewriter," she said calmly. "But maybe I *borrowed* one from NETT a while back. Like last year."

"You stole it."

"Maybe *you* stole it," she countered. "A bad-news kid, bitter about his failed audition, has a temper tantrum and strikes back by wrecking some scenery, then stealing a NETT typewriter that he leaves his fingerprints all over. Then he thinks about it some more and decides to go after bigger fish, huh? Like the director who shut him out, *humiliated* him. After the killing is done, this kid comes back, hits on a veteran NETT actress, and gets himself invited to NETT parties just to see how happy everyone is with his work. How's that?"

Eddie went tense, said, "You're crazy."

Angela slid him a wicked grin. Then she pointed her index finger at him, like the barrel of a gun, and said, "But I do have your number."

"This is all crazy."

"There are layers of understanding here," Angela replied. "Lots of ways to look at this."

"Start with the basics."

"He ignored me," she said.

"Who?"

"Who do you think!"

"Your father."

Angela burst into a cruel snigger. "That goes without saying. I'm talking about my hired father, Sweet Corey." Her darkening blue eyes suddenly glittered with excitement.

"How could he ignore you?"

"Let me put it this way: I loved him, I worked for him, but after a while the only performance he wanted from me and the other girls in the troupe was to play the part of *object*. He stopped talking *to* us, just *at* us, usually *over* us. Sometimes during rehearsal he'd shove us around the stage like furniture."

"That's worse than the boys got?"

"The boys he wanted to control and possess. There's the difference. But what a difference. He didn't want closeness with any of us. He wanted dominance over all of us. With the boys his methods were more . . . specialized."

"So you all joined forces."

"Hardly," Angela said with arrogant contempt.

"Then you did do it, the whole thing?"

"Writer, director, producer . . . executioner," Angela replied brightly.

"No."

"You don't believe me? You should. You better. You *will.*"

Eddie didn't know what to say. He opted again for an attitude. "Convince me," he said, trying for cool, but not quite pulling it off.

"Where should I begin?"

"Start with motive."

"That's easy. First, I wanted to let him know I understood him, I could see through all the games and masks."

"What masks?"

"In his mind I'd become nothing, none of us were."

"The girls, you mean."

"Uh-huh. And when I finally recognized and accepted that, it all fell into place. I knew what I wanted and how to get it."

"What exactly did you want?"

"To reverse the roles permanently. I wanted a controlled situation, a showdown. I wanted him to *see me,* not his image of me. I wanted to force him to acknowledge my talent again, like at the start. I wanted him to *care* about my talent. But mostly I wanted him to suffer for what he'd done, and suffer the same way I did, feel humiliated and terrified and controlled. I wanted to show him he couldn't have his fantasies forever, that they were vulnerable, and my imagination was more powerful than his. I wanted to put him down in some ultimate, permanent way."

"You weren't thinking about the boys."

"Sure I was, but not that much. I mean, what he was doing to them is exactly like what happens to girls, women every day, everywhere."

"Exploitation? Discrimination?" Eddie was trying to be ironic.

"I'm way beyond that," she said. "Because worse than being used is when you're made to feel you *deserve* to be used, there aren't any options. Almost every day he used us and let us know every chance he got we were being used."

"Oh, c'mon," chided Eddie. "Cut the melodrama."

"I mean it!" she yelped, trying to check the doubt in his tone. "He scared me, made me submissive, silent. But then I hit on it, the way to reclaim myself, take back the power." Her cold blue eyes glowed with intensity.

"What're you saying?" asked Eddie, exasperated now. "You actually killed him, *personally*?"

"Only one other thing would've made it perfect," she said, ignoring Eddie's question.

"You hear me?" he asked.

"I wanted to film it, Eddie. The whole thing. I wanted to be able to watch it, see it all every night if I cared to, over and over and over again, just to be sure it really happened, that I really pulled it off. I wanted it to happen and happen and happen. I wanted to totally destroy him."

"Well, didn't you?" asked Eddie, glancing at the

door, anxious now to beat a fast retreat. He didn't know anymore who he was talking to or why he was there.

But Angela jerked him back to the conversation by asking, "You wanna know about 'means'?"

"Sure, why not."

"That was the beautiful thing. I used his own obsessions, his most glaring weakness to do him." Angela stopped, held Eddie's gaze with what was meant to be a chilling look. Which worked.

"Yeah," Eddie managed to mumble.

"I mean, he went out there that night thinking he could have those guys *again*, keep doing it to all of us, you know? Only he didn't realize this time *I* was the director, and the action of the play was all *mine*. Angela's Magic Theater."

Eddie took a deep breath. "So you're admitting you set him up. You got him killed, that's where it's at."

Angela showed him a little smile of superiority, her haunting eyes steady on his face. "That's *exactly* where it's at," she said.

Eddie looked at the door.

"You know how I wanted to do it at first?" she continued.

"Of course not."

"Wanna know?"

"You're going to tell me."

"I planned to shoot him."

"Where?"

"In the head, I suppose. Where'd you think?"

"I meant where would he be that you could shoot him?"

"Right where I wanted him, Orchestra Hall."

Eddie grimaced.

"That was plan A. I'd gotten tickets for most of the NETT parents and staff."

"That cost you."

"Eddie, I have lots of 'discretionary cash,' as Daddy says. I can buy things outright and not leave a trail."

"Then what?"

"Since they'd all be sitting in the same section, I figured I could disguise myself as an usher, move in, zap Corey, and leave him surrounded by enough suspects to keep the cops busy for twenty years. I wanted to use Mr. Russo's gun."

"Who's Mr. Russo?"

"His son was a—"

"Victim," said Eddie, guessing the inevitable.

"Right."

"The kid would give you a gun?"

"Hey, that'd be really clever— Yo, Ricky, can I use your daddy's pistol to punch Corey's ticket?"

"How then?"

"Steal it."

"Did you?"

"I couldn't. Then I saw I didn't have to. There was a better, more interesting and effective way, a way that gave Corey a chance to suffer."

"So how'd you do it, the final run?" asked Eddie. "How'd you get everybody to go along?" He still couldn't believe all she had said, what he was asking.

She studied him a moment. "I'm not telling you absolutely everything," she replied.

"Because you can't."

"Because someday you'll be glad you're ignorant."

"Know what I really think?" ventured Eddie.

"Uh-uh."

"That whatever happened to Howe-Browne happened, and you're just jumping in for the fun of it now, to dramatize yourself."

Immediately Eddie knew he'd said the forbidden thing. Angela shot him a disgusted glare and began breathing faster. "I don't goddam *believe* it!" she shouted.

"Me either," Eddie chipped in.

"I trusted you, with the most important thing I know." She seemed to be coming apart.

"You've recruited an audience for *your* fantasies is what you've done. But the audience can't buy it. The audience is walking out on you," said Eddie.

Angela spun around, strode to her desk, grabbed the handle of the top drawer, seemed about to open it when she stopped, held herself stone still. Then Eddie watched her shoulders begin to quiver, heard the first gulping breath of her crying. He crossed the room and stood behind her, placed his hands gently on her shoulders, sorry he'd hurt her feelings, forgetting for a moment what she'd just confessed.

Before he could speak, she yelled, "Don't *touch* me!" and pulled away from him so fiercely she almost lost her balance. Suddenly her hand came up, slashed at his face, but he caught her wrist and forced it down. When he felt the strength, the rage, drain from her arm he let it go and backed off, his hands dropping to his sides. Her eyes were still ablaze.

"My God, how I trusted you," she said again through clenched teeth. "I thought you'd understand. But I was a fool. And I created a loose end, right?" She glowered at him.

"By now there's lots of loose ends," he said.

She pulled back her shoulders, lifted her head defiantly, her eyes boring into him. "You're wrong," she said coldly. Then an expression he couldn't read, one he'd never seen before, flashed across her face.

"Don't get excited, okay?" he said. "I didn't mean anything." He was trying to stall, come up with a good way to make a graceful, clean escape.

"You're right about that," she said.

"What?"

"You *don't* mean anything."

Eddie shrugged and avoided her gaze. Soon the silence became embarrassing, but Eddie let it stand. Finally he asked, "Why don't you just say it?"

"Say what?" she responded, aiming a phony smile at him.

"About Howe-Browne."

"I put him under," she said without hesitation. "I was the last one to see him alive."

Eddie's mouth hung open.

"It was really a very simple decision," she continued, the smile a faraway one now. "When you believe something must be done, you've got to act on that belief. And doing what you really should do makes you free, okay? I didn't just want to kill him. I *needed* to, for self-preservation."

"You killed another guy, that fisherman."

"An accident. Bad timing on his part and not my problem."

"But you're going to get caught," Eddie said. "Then you won't be free at all. The media won't let this thing fade."

"That's okay. In fact, that'd be wonderful. The more attention paid to my work the better. And the longer it takes them to solve it, the better. So far the only thing they proved is my superiority as a dramatist. They can't find the seams. I'm probably the best there is around here. And in time they'll know it. But none of them can know it now, not just yet anyway."

"But I know."

"At the moment," she said casually.

"This place is dangerous," Eddie muttered.

"Full of exploiters and manipulators who use people," continued Angela with exaggerated irony. "And who must be stopped."

"But it's not your right to stop them."

Now her eyes really drilled into him. "It's my duty," she said. "Besides, he killed himself. When he let his weaknesses control him, when he misused my talent and my love, he condemned himself. He was a petty, self-serving, self-caressing, kinky creep. Mr. Doyle was right. He got better than he deserved."

"And you won't pay for anything."

"I have no debts."

"You're sure you'll get away with it."

"Cleanly."

"How can you be sure?"

"Either they'll never connect me with the thing, or

if someone smart enough gets into it, and they do come after me and charge me, I'll win in court, no sweat."

"Innocent by reason of insanity."

Angela glared at him again, seemed about to really unload, maybe try hitting him again. Instead she let the pause build and then, timing her line perfectly, announced, "Innocent by killing in self-defense. And remember—I always have you to throw at them."

Eddie let the implications of that comment gather and sink into his mind. His only response was, "I think I better go."

Angela said, "You're already gone."

After taking a step toward the door, Eddie spun around and blurted, "You killed your brother, too!"

Showing no emotion, making no gesture, Angela replied, "He's dead."

Eddie took a quick breath and hurried out of the room.

chapter 15

The moment Eddie hit the street in front of Angela's house, he began running. He ran until his T-shirt was sweat stained on the chest and back. He ran down alleys, cutting back and forth through strange neighborhoods, trying to make sure no one followed him.

Finally, he felt safe enough to slow down, to walk, to start thinking. He realized it was time to go to Aunt Cyn with the problem of Angela Favor. Probably past the time. But he knew she wouldn't be home till after supper. She was "meeting a friend," something Eddie wished he could do that second.

Instead he wandered aimlessly for an hour trying to clear his mind, set things straight. Only Angela kept haunting him. Her anger. That's what impressed Eddie

—the depth, the intensity of her frustration and anger. From what Eddie could tell, Angela thought she'd been betrayed by everybody she was supposed to be able to trust. And with nobody to stand up for her, she'd decided to stand up for herself, win herself back from everyone who took advantage, especially Corey Howe-Browne. She'd trusted him too much with what was most important to her. But she also trusted *me*, thought Eddie. That's what she'd said.

Recalling her words made Eddie shudder. Suddenly he realized how vulnerable he was, out here on the street with no money, no protection. He was thinking now of the cash he had hidden in his room, $290, and the limerick sheets he'd taken from Angela's wastebasket. He had to have those. He needed the security. So he ran back to Cyn's.

Standing at Cynthia's front door, Eddie felt wary, anxious. Things weren't right. First, the "secret" spare key (taped under the mailbox) was in the lock. And the front door was ajar. There were no lights on or sounds in the house. Cyn had classical music playing at low volume nearly every afternoon.

Eddie gently pushed the door open and listened. There was only silence. He called Cyn's name but got no response. Finally, he decided to race to his closet, grab the valuables, and run again.

He charged in, hurried to his room, threw on the lights, and groaned. There on his desk sat the Smith-

Corona Coronet Super 12 that Angela had used to type any number of incriminating documents. A page was in it now.

Eddie felt panic spreading through his chest.

He grabbed at the typewriter and yanked out the sheet. On it he read:

Dear Detective Crenshaw:

You think now you're closing the gap,
And you'll soon nab a guy for the zap
That put Corey away
On a cold winter's day,
But I still better draw you a map.

Forget the wimp and the whiner.
Their parts in the play were quite minor.
So look for a judge
With a helluva grudge
And the brains to put Corey supiner.

Maybe I'm no poet, but I am very truly yours,
The Top E-Lim-inator!
(cc to Crenshaw and E-File)

Eddie moaned and stuffed the new limericks in his jeans pocket. Then he picked up the typewriter with both hands and looked for a place to throw it, hide it. He felt ridiculous because he couldn't see how to rid himself of the thing, the *real* evidence. Maybe he could take it to a dumpster, toss it in. Then the thought clutched him that maybe Crenshaw had already seen these limericks. Angela certainly knew how to time such things, so maybe Crenshaw or some other cop was already here, in the house, waiting to bust him. The front door had been open. . . .

Before Eddie could react, make a move to get the typewriter out of his room, out of his life, Aunt Cyn returned.

She called to him from the front hall. "Eddie? Hey, don't leave the key in the door, okay? Eddie?"

Eddie didn't answer.

"Eddie?" Cyn persisted, her tone more cautious now, troubled.

Eddie quickly slid the typewriter under his bed and went into the closet after his money and Angela's other writings. When he came stumbling, rushing out he ran right into the ACE.

"You didn't hear me?" she asked.

Eddie shrugged, tried to smile.

"What's going on?"

"Nothing," he said, looking down at his desk top, reaching over to straighten some perfectly straight note-books.

"Why'd you leave the front door open with the key in it?"

"Well, I . . . I kind of had to get to the bathroom," he improvised.

Eddie's lie was cut short by the doorbell.

Cynthia shot him a what-the-heck, bunched-eye-brows look and called down the hall, "Just a minute." She left Eddie's room to answer the door.

Eddie followed her for two long strides, then veered into her study, where he could get a peek at their visitor from one of the big front windows. Pulling the curtain edge back, Eddie couldn't believe his eyes. It was Crenshaw! Saying something to Cyn about an anonymous phone call, a tip. Asking to see a guy named Edrich Lymurek.

Eddie didn't wait to hear more. Instead he stepped quickly back into his room and closed the door. He checked his pockets for the drafts of Angela's limericks. As he stared at the papers he wondered what good they were to him now. How could he prove Angela had typed them? That he hadn't? Especially now that the damn Corona was under his bed. How'd she know about the key? Eddie wondered. How'd she know about *everything*?

Truly frightened, Eddie flicked off the lights and went for the bedroom window facing the backyard. He hurriedly raised the sash, unhooked the old wooden screen, and popped it open. Even though the ground was a good eight or nine feet below, Eddie took his chances, swiftly working himself through the window and out of the room.

He dropped to the dirt while the screen swung back into place with a dull thud. He didn't wait to see if the noise had given him away. Instead he was off and running once more, knowing now that Crenshaw could put him into the case for keeps.

Just as he left the yard, Eddie pulled up, asked himself why the hell he hadn't taken the damn typewriter with him. His fingerprints were all over it again, undoubtedly the only prints they'd find. He glanced back at his bedroom window just in time to see Crenshaw flip the lights on and start looking around. Eddie shook his head and stepped into the shadows.

A little later, Crenshaw stood before the front door of Angela Favor's house, holding his finger on the bell. He'd missed the Lymurek kid, but the aunt had been most helpful. Together they'd found the typewriter, though she claimed—and very convincingly—that she'd never seen it before. Then she told him about young Eddie and mysterious Angela. Crenshaw wasn't surprised by the information because Angela Favor had been on his mind for a while now.

Ringing the bell again, Crenshaw knew someone was home. He'd heard a door slam inside, the scuffle of footsteps moving across hardwood floors. As he stood there, he started thinking about how much time he spent on doorsteps waiting for people to open up to him.

That afternoon, the last thing Crenshaw had said before leaving his colleagues in the squad room was, "You guys know what I got here, after talking to all those kids? Can you see it? I got half-a-dozen accessories, but no killer. I got guys tying him up wearing costumes, who then split. I got a hooded chanter who reads Howe-Browne his 'Condemnation Proclamation.' Then the kid burns it and doesn't remember what it said because he only saw the thing once, and he disappears. Another guy, sixteen, wearing a tuxedo and a Ronald Reagan rubber head, drives Howe-Browne's car three miles to a deserted side road and leaves it there and gets picked up. Then *poof*! I got no one left who can put somebody in the car with Corey after that. I've got nobody who can finger the crazy that put the car in the lake."

But now, at last, he felt he was getting close. And his instinct kept telling him this girl, this Angela Favor, had come up in way too many of his conversations with the boys at NETT. Whenever Crenshaw had asked about other NETT students who seemed particularly resentful toward Howe-Browne, or especially interested in the experiences of the boys Crenshaw was questioning, Angela Favor's name made every list.

Crenshaw had tried interviewing the other girls in the troupe, but surprisingly they had little to tell. They said they weren't particularly close to Angela Favor. The girl was a loner. But a talent, they gave her that.

And now there was a sort of sudden boyfriend, Edrich Lymurek. When the aunt gave him a picture of the kid, Crenshaw remembered seeing him at a rehearsal. He'd noticed Edrich noticing him, watching him. So Lymurek might be a way in. He'd get to him soon enough. The boy couldn't go very far. He was broke, according to the aunt.

Finally, Angela responded and snapped open the lock. When she finished pulling back the heavy front door, Crenshaw was momentarily stunned. Before him stood an exquisitely made-up, strikingly dressed young woman who looked a good ten years older than the sixteen she was supposed to be. Her beauty was downright intimidating—silky jet-black hair, crystal blue eyes, high cheekbones, arrogantly arched brows.

"Yes?" she said at last. "What is it?"

Crenshaw was fumbling for his shield when he managed to reply, "I'd like to ask you some questions about your relationship with the New Energy Theater Troupe, and a boy."

"I imagine," Angela said coyly. "How come?"

"This young man you're friends with?" Crenshaw replied, working the badge out at last, flashing it at Angela. "I'm Detective—"

"Robert Crenshaw," finished Angela. "Everyone with a TV knows that."

Crenshaw nodded. "May I come in?"

"My parents aren't home. And I'm already late." She glanced at her watch.

"Oh."

"Might look funny, you know, me inviting you in."

Crenshaw caught a glimpse of her ironic smile just before it disappeared. He knew she was putting him on but didn't know what to do about it.

"And I can't imagine why you need me," Angela continued before Crenshaw could speak.

Crenshaw began a long, slow smile. She was some actress, he thought. She had what the professionals call *presence*. "About this boy you know."

"From NETT, I suppose. Who?"

"Young man named Edrich Lymurek."

Angela offered a confused look, her forehead lined with wrinkles of concentration. "You mean the guy they call Eddie Limerick?" she asked.

"I guess," said Crenshaw.

Angela replied, "I barely know him, really."

* * *

Eddie couldn't believe his luck. He'd never gotten such fast service when he'd really, badly, desperately needed a ride. Hitchhiking in rain, snow, or heat had never inspired many grim-faced drivers to empathize with him, offer a lift. But this time, after only a ten-minute wait on Lyndale Avenue, he'd caught a ride with a sales rep who'd driven into the city from Glencoe, a town seventy miles to the southwest of Minneapolis.

After the generous sales rep—"Call me Jimbob, huh?"—had dropped him off in downtown Glencoe, Eddie decided it would be best to keep moving, make another town or two before he packed it in for the night. He thought if they were trying to find him and gave his picture to the TV guys, ol' "Call me Jimbob" would easily identify him and probably call first chance he got, Mr. Good Citizen, and ruin Eddie's streak. So he headed out of town on foot, hoping to obscure and complicate his trail. The fading spring sky was clear, the air fresh and warm. He felt clean. He knew he could walk a long time before he got too hungry or too tired to continue.

But once more he didn't have to walk far. He was on the outskirts of Glencoe when a semiretired farmer, in his eighties, it looked like, offered him a ride in the bed of his old pickup truck. He wanted to let Eddie in the cab, but the passenger's side was filled with potted plants. That lift took him all the way to little Stewart, Minnesota, where Eddie decided he'd run enough for one day. He felt suddenly famished and fatigued. He asked the farmer for the name and location of a cheap motel.

"You'll be looking for the Joy," said the old man with a wink. "Eight dollars a night still. Pretty basic."

"Where is it?"

"Out to the southwest there," he said pointing. "Not all that far."

Eddie thanked him and started walking. On his way to the Joy Motel he passed a truck-stop café, where he sat down just long enough for a bowl of homemade chili and a Coke.

As for the Joy Motel, it was a little pink six-unit affair no longer on a main highway, only two cars dozing in the weed-filled gravel parking lot. My kind of place, thought Eddie, as he approached the end unit and the door marked OFFICE. Inside a pleasant grandmother-type in a faded housecoat took his nine dollars ("Inflation, honey," she explained) and sent him to unit five.

His room was well worn, tacky and shabby, but basically clean and basically basic. Eddie couldn't have cared less. He was tired now, sure he'd sleep like a dead man. He locked and chained the door, kicked off his shoes, and lay down on the stiff twin mattress. He laced his hands behind his head, closed his eyes, listened to the faraway hum and wooosh of the occasional cars passing by the Joy Motel. He wanted to slide into the deep sleep he needed and deserved.

But hard as he tried, it wouldn't come. He couldn't sleep because his mind kept racing, kept him thinking about everybody, everything that had troubled him lately, changed his life completely in less than two weeks. He thought about Angela and felt a strange sympathy for the tragedy of her situation, the waste of her talent, the torment of her future. But then he remembered what Alex James had told him, that Angela didn't just get caught up in tragedy—she seemed to create it.

Next, Aunt Cynthia crossed his mind, and he tried to figure what she'd be thinking about him right now. Would she be so disappointed and embarrassed by his actions that she'd never speak to him again? Would he become just another Bobby Lymurek in her eyes? Maybe. And if so, he deserved Cynthia's scorn and rejection. Then Eddie recalled Moses Goldman and some of the things he'd said about social responsibility and moral decision making. And before long Eddie began wondering how far he'd have to run to escape what he *knew*.

What he didn't know was what to do about his feelings, his doubts, his suspicions. He wondered what the police thought by now. Had Angela given Crenshaw her complete frame-up story about him? Had she herself confessed? Then he thought, Maybe she didn't really have anything to confess. Maybe he'd been right in the first place and it was *show time* all along, just another chance for her to promote herself, play a role. That notion consoled Eddie for a moment, until he remembered his "evidence."

So he thought, Suppose I go to Crenshaw with what I have. What would happen then? I'd look like an idiot is what would happen, he concluded. In reality, he had no proof of anything.

But he knew in his heart she'd done it, that she'd

set up everybody to play her game, even him. Magic Theater, she'd called it. At first Eddie had been cast in the role of audience/confidant. He was there to recognize and appreciate the complexity and sophistication and cleverness of Angela's "play." Ultimately, his part was *fall guy.* Eddie shook his head, stunned and impressed by Angela's intelligence, her resourcefulness. She apparently could take whatever came her way and make it work for her.

And at that precise moment, when that insight bore into his mind, Eddie realized fully and vividly what Angela had been trying to tell him: She didn't think she was smarter, more talented and creative, than just Corey Howe-Browne; she thought she was smarter than everyone. And maybe she was. After all, as things were turning out, everyone connected with NETT was a suspect, but no one was a real prospect as a suspect . . . except Eddie. She'd trapped him in a hall of mirrors, and everywhere he looked he saw only himself in a crowd of distorted strangers.

Eddie sat up slowly on the bed, swung his feet onto the floor, tried to figure out the best way to do whatever he decided to do. He had to defend himself, cut his name decisively from Crenshaw's suspect list. But despite everything, he also felt some responsibility for Angela, for whatever else she might do if he didn't come forward.

Besides, if he kept doing what he was starting to do at the Joy Motel—running and hiding from his problems—who could he *possibly* become but Bobby Lymurek? And if all he accomplished was to get Angela some real help, he would've done more for her than anyone had done for either of them. She was like him in so many ways, he realized. That scared him. She scared him. And he didn't want to go on being afraid of losing himself by default—because he didn't have the guts to stand up and do what was necessary. He thought if he could help her at all, he'd be helping himself in some long-term, permanent way.

Eventually, he put on his shoes and started for the door. It was late, but maybe not too late. He walked out of the Joy with no clear idea of how he could save himself, let alone Angela Favor.

Still in his office, long after the other guys on his shift had gone home, Robert Crenshaw stared at his notes on the Howe-Browne case. He was thinking that in his seventeen years of police work he'd seen it all. Until this thing came along. By now he was pretty sure he knew what had happened. Someone, maybe this girl Angela, maybe a committee, had contacted and recruited only those boys who were most deeply involved and whose parents were the most dangerously bitter and outspoken. Then, with a clarity and simplicity of purpose so pure it rivaled anything he'd heard of, a scenario had been set up so complex, so intricately reflexive, that anywhere he turned, looking for a way out or into the structure, led nowhere and everywhere, a classic labyrinth.

He still thought this Lymurek kid was a key, maybe the direct link, and he hoped they'd pick him up soon. The girl had tried hard to cover for him, denying her relationship with him, but that, of course, made him all the more suspect, more important to question. And the boy did have the machine, the Smith-Corona.

The father hatred implicit in the act of killing Howe-Browne was also on Crenshaw's mind, an angle he wanted to work. He learned from the aunt that Edrich Lymurek and his father had a terrible relationship. But Crenshaw had also discovered stressed relations between nearly all of the NETT kids and their dads. Doyle and Caine and Russo, and even the girl, Angela Favor. Verbal and some physical abuse were the norm. Crenshaw knew R. Todd Favor by reputation and was just now getting a sense of the man's life at home.

Maybe he'd call in a shrink, run a few things by him.

But before doing any of that he needed to see Edrich Lymurek. There were just too many helpful things happening at once, and all the tips and clues and cues leading to Lymurek were too easy, too convenient, too well-timed to satisfy Crenshaw's instincts. So he had to find him very soon.

He sighed.

The young man would turn up eventually, concluded Crenshaw, as he switched off his desk lamp and stood. They always do.

By nine o'clock the following morning, Eddie was there, across the street from Crenshaw's precinct building. Eddie stood inside a phone booth, the receiver in one hand, a quarter in the other. Already he'd seen Crenshaw report in and disappear through the station's big double doors. So all Eddie had to do now was decide, choose whether or not to become even more involved in the case, make it truly his case, or write the whole thing off, pack up, and run forever. What nagged him was the fear that he had no options, that for him it was already too late.

Suddenly, he wished he could slide down in the booth and fall asleep and then wake up to find it all had been a dream, a nightmare. But he knew that wouldn't, couldn't happen. It would be a stupid ending anyway, one that's been wished before and never ever worked. Instead, he dropped the coin into the phone and accepted his responsibility.

chapter 16

The phone at the precinct rang and rang. Finally someone answered, grunted out the precinct number, sounded
irritated and impatient, like he was doing Eddie a big
favor by taking the call. Eddie bristled but managed to
say, "Detective Crenshaw, please."

"He's in a meeting till noon. Call back later."

And before Eddie could ask to leave a message, the
guy hung up.

Eddie slammed the receiver back in the cradle. He
had no more quarters. And he suddenly had no more
desire to help Crenshaw solve his problem. He stepped
out of the booth and started walking.

He knew he should go back to Cynthia's and explain
where he'd been and what he'd gotten caught up in. But
he couldn't see doing that either. He remembered from

TV and movies how the cops always staked out your address, hoping you'd be stupid enough to go there. Besides, Eddie needed more time to work out where he stood and what he could do about it.

So he kept moving, walking at a brisk clip, feeling surprisingly alert and energetic, despite his nearly sleepless night. He drifted closer to downtown, stopped for lunch at a fast-food place, spent an hour browsing in a bookstore that specialized in mysteries, then headed toward Nicollet High School. He went there with no other plans than to find a pickup game. He needed to play again. He hoped that would give some rhythm to his thinking.

By the time he reached Nicollet, school was out and the game was going. Even from nearly a block away Eddie could see that they were all there, including Alex. But he wanted to play, so not even his apprehension about Alex stopped him.

When Eddie was close enough to be spotted by Willis, the game stopped. One of the guards, Jay-Jay, held the ball, and all of the guys stared at Eddie, frozen in place. Finally, Willis walked over to him.

"Hey, Limerick man, how you doin'?" Willis asked pleasantly. "You been away, huh?"

"Yeah," Eddie replied. Meeting Willis's gaze, he asked, "You need another guy?"

"No, not today."

"Next game?"

"Don't think so, man."

"What's the deal?"

"All spots taken, you know?"

"No," said Eddie, "I don't know."

"We got our quota," Willis pointed out.

That's when Eddie saw the big white kid playing opposite Birch. Eddie looked at Willis, who wasn't smiling.

"Not a personal thing, man," said Willis.

"I don't get it."

"Loyalty thing. A respect thing. Alex, you know."

"He doesn't like me, that's his problem. Doesn't mean we can't get along enough to play ball."

"Oh, but it does, Limerick. An' you're wrong, baby. *Is* your problem. That what he sees anyway."

"*He* sees. Alex?"

"He think you better decide, man. Real soon."

"Decide what?"

"If you be movin' in with the Angel, or clear on out like you got some brains."

"I'm not seeing her anymore," said Eddie. "I'm through."

Willis looked genuinely surprised, said, "Oh, yeah?" Then he looked toward Alex and added, "Well, he don't know that."

Eddie concluded, "We all gotta talk. I mean, I need your advice."

After Eddie had convinced Alex and Willis that he, too, now believed Angela was both dangerous and very sick, they thought he should go to Crenshaw with it.

"The man's real smart, even if he workin' for the home team," said Willis.

Alex made only one comment: "When they finally bust her ass, make sure I get in on it. Even jus' to watch."

Eddie said sure, thinking, *Everybody's* angry here. Willis said, "Be good," as Eddie started off, supposedly heading for a showdown with Crenshaw. Eddie didn't know how to interpret the remark.

But Eddie thought an explanation, a confession to Cynthia should be the next showdown. He hurried toward her place, ready to confide what he knew and thought about Angela Favor, no matter who was waiting for him.

Eddie knocked first and then let himself in. His aunt met him in the hallway. "You're back," she said matter-of-factly.

"Yeah," Eddie mumbled. "Sorry."

"Forget sorry, okay? I don't need that. I need somebody I can trust around here, somebody with enough respect to trust me."

"I need to trust you now," Eddie replied.

"I bet you do," she answered. Before Eddie could go on she asked, "Where'd you get the typewriter?"

Eddie shook his head slowly, then began telling about Angela. He ended his story with, "It comes down to my word against hers. I mean, I thought I had something on her, but she planted everything I have. She gave it to me as part of a setup. And I don't know how to prove that."

"There must be something," Cyn replied. "She

couldn't possibly know what you were doing that particular night."

"Don't underestimate her."

"You're right to go to Crenshaw. The police have the resources to check all the details."

"I hope so," said Eddie.

Cynthia nodded thoughtfully before saying, "There's something else you should know."

Eddie was caught off balance again.

"What?" he asked.

"Your father called. He wants to talk to you, wants you back with him."

"No way!" said Eddie, fuming and striding off. "No *way*," he repeated. "I'm not going near him."

"Eddie—"

"*Anywhere* he is. Ever again!"

"Eddie . . ."

The words came rushing out. "He's sick and I can't help him, not by going back or anything else. So I won't do it. I can't!"

Cynthia looked at him anxiously, then came close to him, extending her arms. He let her embrace him. But soon he was hugging her back, fighting off the tears, tears of exhaustion, shock, fear, and confusion. Cynthia whispered, "That's okay, Eddie. Everything's okay. Let it go."

And he did. All the anxieties and apprehensions he'd been repressing for years stormed to the surface, raced through his heart and mind, and poured out his eyes. And all the while, his aunt Cynthia Edrich did what no one else had ever thought to do—she held him, stood up for him, and held on.

chapter 17

Eddie had held his eyes on Crenshaw the whole time he told his story. Crenshaw kept nodding and nodding, encouraging Eddie to go on, but saying very little himself. When Eddie finally presented his "evidence," Crenshaw didn't even blink, just took the papers and hummed something to himself. At that point Eddie had to ask, "You believe any of this?"

"Oh, I believe almost everything, son."

"Why?"

"Why not? You're making as much sense as anyone else in this case."

"So it's useless," Eddie speculated.

"Let's put it this way—you're confirming some of our suspicions, things we've gotten from other sources."

"You already know about her?" Eddie asked, incredulous.

"And about you," Crenshaw said ominously. "But her name comes up far more often." Crenshaw looked very closely now at the limerick fragments.

"What're you going to do?" Eddie asked, interrupting Crenshaw's exploration.

"Talk to a guy," said Crenshaw.

Before Eddie could say anything else Crenshaw was up and signaling for Eddie to follow him out of the office. "Sit over there," Crenshaw said, pointing to a sort of waiting-room area with a couch and end table. On the table Eddie spotted a pile of ragged magazines. He walked over to the couch and sat down.

Crenshaw and Dr. Duane McDowell, psychiatrist, had already had several interesting conversations about this case, about the father problems common to the NETT victims, about Angela Favor's potential for involvement in the Howe-Browne and Kozlicki murders. But those talks were merely imaginative and speculative. With the information the Lymurek kid had just brought in, everything changed. Their conjectures could become more focused, more real. The moment Crenshaw had picked up the phone and found Eddie on the other end, dying to talk about Angela Favor, Crenshaw had directed an aide to contact McDowell.

As Crenshaw finished retelling Eddie's story to the psychiatrist, both men understood the situation. Both had come to the same conclusion.

"If it's really Angela Favor, you aren't going to catch her, Robert," said McDowell, a tall, muscular former college quarterback.

"You mean we can arrest but never convict her," said Crenshaw.

"Not for Howe-Browne."

"I wouldn't be so sure," Crenshaw grunted. He looked down at the scratch pad he was supposedly taking notes on. "She put on a show when I talked to her, really got into her charm thing, but we didn't have Lymurek then. I'd like to see how she reacts to Edrich's story."

"Robert, even if she *confesses*, she seems smart enough to slip by with some sort of insanity defense, as clichéd as that sounds."

"But you think it's her."

"I think she'd have a lot to gain in her mind if Howe-Browne were destroyed. Based on what your new witness just told you anyway."

"Elaborate," said Crenshaw.

"It's all quite ironic," commented McDowell.

"Let's skip ironic," Crenshaw replied. "Ironic ain't gonna play too well, Doc."

"What I meant was that Angela Favor and Howe-Browne appear to be far more alike than different."

Crenshaw looked over at McDowell. "Explain," he prompted.

"People like them, people who know they've got a special talent, a perspective that's original and singular, when such people find a place, an activity, an outlet for their talent, that's the only time they experience any real pleasure. And the pleasure is the kind that comes from playing close to the edge, to danger, the danger of failure. So if life is going particularly well, they sometimes can't help complicating things, just to maintain the tension they need to live."

"You know who you're describing?" asked Crenshaw.

McDowell shook his head.

"Our boy Edrich. Check out his record." Crenshaw shoved the file he had on Eddie across the desk.

McDowell scanned it. Nodding, he said, "No matter where you turn, Robert, there's the father angle. Am I right?"

"Yessir," sighed Crenshaw, "there certainly is the father angle. The controller, the oppressor."

"Or the isolated, frustrated, and fearful. The unloved," McDowell suggested. "It's not easy being a dad."

Crenshaw reflected on that a moment, then said, "Is everybody crazy, Doc?"

McDowell smiled. "When you find a young person angry enough to kill somebody, you don't have to look at him—or her—very long before you see Mom or Dad staring back at you."

Crenshaw looked off but said nothing.

"Lymurek's story opens things up, though," the doctor added.

"More like closes things down," Crenshaw replied, meeting McDowell's stare. "But maybe not for a jury of our peers." He paused, then added, "It won't be easy getting her to tell it all again, is what I'm thinking."

"I said you'll never really nail her with this. If she's the one."

"Well, she looks awfully good for it at the moment, Doc. I mean that typewriter was stolen from the NETT school over a year ago, and it's definitely the one the poetry was typed on. We just haven't found someone who can put her at the keys typing the stuff."

"She can't be allowed to run around loose," said McDowell.

"That's right."

"She needs help."

"Uh-huh. Don't we all."

Both men were quiet for a few moments, contemplating the situation. Then McDowell roused himself and said, "I'm all for public service, Robert, but I've got a private practice that says I'm late for my next appointment."

Crenshaw stood up, thanked McDowell for coming in on such short notice. After the doctor had left, Crenshaw sat down and began drawing diagrams, a sort of family tree of motivations, causes and effects. He wanted to see as clearly as possible why he was sure Angela Favor's confession to Lymurek was perfectly accurate and logical given her present circumstances and past experience. He wanted to feel that his inclination to go for a single startling face-off with her was the best strategy. Because this girl was certainly no Tommy Doyle and couldn't be dealt with the same way. Angela Favor had tons of self-confidence. She demanded an especially imaginative effort from Crenshaw if he was ever to catch her off balance. Crenshaw was deep in thought when he remembered that Eddie Lymurek was still waiting in the reception area. He hoped.

∗　∗　∗

Crenshaw was glad to find him there, patiently reading a *Sports Illustrated*. He called to him and signaled for him to come back to the office.

"What'd you say she called her project?" asked Crenshaw, closing the door gently, pointing Eddie to a chair.

"The Howe-Browne thing?"

"Yes."

"Angela's Magic Theater."

Crenshaw nodded. "Maybe," he began, "we can do that, too."

"What?"

"Some magic theater. Upset her on her home court, you know?"

"I don't understand," said Eddie.

"If you're not lying, and we'll know shortly if you are, then we have some idea what she did."

"Uh-huh."

"But right now we can't prove it, can't place her at the scene the night he died, can't put her anywhere near the car."

Eddie glanced aside.

"In fact, superficially she's got as much on you as you do on her."

That brought Eddie's startled eyes back to Crenshaw.

"Your word against hers," Crenshaw added. Then, looking at Eddie's file, he said, "And you've got some strikes."

"Like what?" asked Eddie.

"Tell me about your NETT audition."

Eddie dropped his gaze.

"Five hundred dollars' worth of damage to scenery, it says here."

"Wasn't that much," Eddie answered defensively.

"Starts to look like a motive, though."

"Angela thought so, too."

Crenshaw nodded, a trace of a smile changing the mood. "She's plenty observant and resourceful," he declared. "And between you, who's gonna appear more credible in a courtroom? Who can act most believably?"

"I'm hurtin'," Eddie concluded.

"Where were you the night Howe-Browne died, March fifteenth?"

"How should I know?" Eddie answered. "That's a long time ago."

"You want to know?"

Eddie looked anxiously at Crenshaw.

"You were in Rochester playing basketball, riding the bench against John Marshall High School until the fourth quarter."

Eddie said, "I was?"

"According to this box score." Crenshaw held up a Xeroxed copy of a sports page.

"I remember Marshall," Eddie said. "I scored, right?"

"Ten points. Hot shooting for one quarter. And you guys won."

"The last game I played in at Parker."

"It's also called an alibi."

"What about the typewriter?" asked Eddie. "How can I explain that?"

"We're working on it," said Crenshaw.

"Some setup," Eddie commented.

"And don't I wish we had one."

"One what?"

"A good setup, some good theater."

"Why? I thought you couldn't get her for Howe-Browne."

"I think we can get her for *you*," Crenshaw replied, dead serious.

Eddie let his mouth sag open trying to make sense of the remark. "You mean entrapment or something?"

"Uh-uh, no. Not entrapment," said Crenshaw. "Call it an opportunity for clarification."

Eddie thought about it, then said, "But why should you believe me, trust me with all this?"

Crenshaw leaned toward Eddie. "I like how you play under pressure," he said.

Eddie paused again before responding. "What's the plan?" he asked.

"First, I should ask you one more question."

"Okay."

"What about school? Aren't you supposed to be in school?"

"That's two questions," Eddie said, relaxed now, confident he could trust himself to Crenshaw.

Crenshaw regarded Eddie for a moment. "You're pretty tough, huh."

"No."

"But you're tough enough to bring her out in the open, right?"

"You want me for bait?"

"Not exactly. It's just that you're the one she chose to trust. She's invested a lot in you. And if she gets to thinking about how risky it is having you on the loose, considering what you know, she might get real desperate again. Understand?"

"Come after me, you mean?"

"More than that."

Eddie shrugged.

"So we've got to move on her first. Take the offensive."

"How?" asked Eddie.

Crenshaw smiled, then said, "Here's an idea."

chapter 18

It took him two long days, but Crenshaw thought he finally had things set. It hadn't been easy to talk some of them into participating. Others jumped at the chance, glad to find something to do that would end the business. The fathers were the most difficult, one in particular. Yet they surprised Crenshaw with their seemingly genuine concern, their desire to do the right thing finally.

"All comin' down tonight," Crenshaw said to himself, checking his roster once more.

It was well past ten when the actors and actresses began streaming out of the NETT complex, leaving the theater promptly. Angela wasn't suspicious when the director caught up to her halfway down the center aisle and called her aside. She hoped Ward wasn't about to begin one of his rambling philosophical commentaries. He did that sometimes after really good rehearsals or really bad ones, pulled somebody in and used him or her as a sounding board. It was an inside joke at NETT. And tonight's practice had been particularly sharp.

"What is it?" she asked.

Lawrence Ward said, "There's somebody in the office who wants to talk to you."

Now Angela was suspicious. "Who?" she asked. "I mean, it's so late," she added.

"C'mon," said Ward.

He turned toward the office, which was behind the stage, but Angela didn't follow.

"Who is it?" she asked again.

When Ward faced her but said nothing, Angela declared, "I'm going home."

And that's when the lights went out.

"What's going on?" yelled Angela.

Ward still said nothing. Angela didn't even know where he was.

"Ward?" she called out. "C'mon, knock it off, huh? I'm not up for this. I'm tired. Ward?" Then she heard the theater doors being closed and locked. Even in total darkness, she made a run for the nearest exit, but she was too late. "Dammit!" she hollered. "Turn on the damn lights! Ward!"

Just then a single spot lit up center stage. Next, Crenshaw and Tommy Doyle came out and sat down on chairs they carried with them. Angela pushed at the door again, rattled it fiercely, panicking at last.

"No way out, miss," said Crenshaw.

Tommy Doyle stared at her, his jaws clenched.

Angela stopped banging on the door, took a deep breath, and spun around to face Crenshaw. She came a few steps closer. "What the hell is this?" she called. "You've got no right—"

"We have to talk, Angela," interrupted Crenshaw.

"Oh, yeah? About what?"

Crenshaw answered, "Thought you and Tommy here might reminisce about old times is all."

"Right, *Detective*," said Angela, her cool building by the second. "You'll have to do better than wimpy Tommy," she added.

"Really," said Crenshaw.

"Really," she echoed.

"You mean find a better link connecting you to the trouble 'round here?"

Angela said nothing.

"How about this young man?"

Crenshaw looked to his right and Alex James stepped into the spotlight and stood behind Tommy. Angela muttered a half word before she cut herself off. For onstage, another tall, handsome black guy had joined Alex, holding onto his arm—Adrian, the once-talented brother.

Adrian's eyes drifted around the darkened theater, a mindless smile on his face. But when Angela said, "Hi, Adrian," he flinched, hunched closer to Alex.

Alex blurted, "Shut up!"

Crenshaw raised a hand in warning, but Alex couldn't help himself. He went on. "You don't even know he can't talk, right? Never once ask how he's doin'. Never call him once, beg his forgiveness. Never nothin'! You ever think 'bout anything but you? Like what you *stole* from him? We know you set him up," Alex concluded. He turned and put a hand on Adrian's shoulder. "We know it."

Very softly Angela said, "I couldn't help that."

Crenshaw chimed in with, "You want to hear ol' Mark Millerin's version? He thinks you could've helped. Thinks you could've prevented the whole ugly thing, is what he thinks. But you see Mark's not here tonight," Crenshaw explained. "Considering the company already present, I feared for his safety."

"Oh please," said Angela, feisty again, putting on a good show of impatience. "Could we just end this pointless routine and go home? What're you trying to prove?"

"I think you know exactly what I'm trying to prove, Angela," said Crenshaw. "And I think *you think* you're the only one who knows exactly what happened to Mr. Howe-Browne." Crenshaw let the silence simmer dramatically before adding, "But you're not the only one."

Angela reached for the back of an aisle seat for support. "What're you talking about?" she persisted.

Crenshaw looked to the left and Lee Caine walked into the light. He turned and faced Angela and said, "I saw you at the lake that night. I really did."

"*C'mon*, Detective!" groaned Angela. "What a waste of time!" Once again she had bounced back off the ropes swinging. "That lying whiner would say anything to save himself."

The wimp and the whiner, thought Crenshaw, recalling the newest limericks Eddie had found in the type-writer.

Then he heard Angela asking Lee Caine, "And how'd you manage to get from your little costume party way out to Lake Minnetonka in time to see Corey?"

"The same way I got to the house—my snowmobile. I didn't follow all your stupid directions. Not everybody is as stupid as you think," he added with emotion. "I saw you!" he said again.

"Like hell," Angela replied evenly.

"It could be the truth, miss," said Crenshaw. "Isn't that scary?"

An agonizing quiet settled over the procedings. Finally Crenshaw broke it with, "We have a case, miss. We've got these people here, and a few others who know quite a bit. For example," said Crenshaw looking offstage again.

And Eddie made his appearance, walking out to join the others.

Angela greeted him with a sarcastic laugh. "Like old times, huh, killer?" she said. "You're a piece of popcorn, right?" she went on. "About to explode into a nice, white, puffy treat."

Eddie was stunned. She had mouthed Corey's lines almost perfectly.

"You'll never make it, killer," Angela persisted. "You're out of your league."

"You're out of your mind," answered Eddie, the comment slipping by before he could stop himself.

Angela stared at him, slack jawed, her eyes widening in anger, maybe fright.

"You shut your lying mouth!" she screamed. "All of you! Just shut the hell up! And get off my stage!" she cried, coming closer.

Crenshaw stood up and said, "Okay, Angela. Have it your way." Then he signaled for the others to follow him offstage. As they stepped out of the single spot, the light faded quickly and again the theater was dark. This time Angela did no yelling.

Eddie was listening intently in the blackness, trying to hear her footsteps, if she was going for one of the other doors. He heard nothing. She must have been standing still, waiting for the next act. Not even Eddie knew what that was going to involve. But Crenshaw had promised a surprise mystery guest.

Just then the spot flashed on again and who should be sitting in the only chair left on stage but R. Todd Favor.

The next words came from Angela and cut through Eddie like a cold, wet wind.

"You hypocritical bastard!" she hissed.

He lifted his chin, stared out at her, gave her a small nod. "Probably," he said. "But I want to help, I—"

"Like hell," Angela countered. "But hey," she continued, "where's everybody else? Where's Momsy?"

R. Todd Favor cleared his throat and said, "Mother couldn't make it, I'm sorry. And, of course, Kevin—"

Angela shrieked, "Shut up! Just shut up about him! I didn't do anything to him! Why won't you believe me? I mean, what do you want?"

"I want to help," said Angela's father, looking away.

"*Help?*" roared Angela. "The only reason you're here is to cover your ass!"

"I want to help," he repeated less fervently now.

"All you had to do was *listen*, Daddy! Just pay some *attention*, see what's really happening!"

R. Todd Favor brought his troubled gaze back to Angela and they locked stares. Then slowly, clearly, enunciating each word so that his anger and frustration were unmistakable, he said, "See and pay attention to *what?*"

"I didn't do it, Daddy!" Angela blurted. "I didn't kill him!"

"You've said that before. I—"

"You *never* believe in me!"

"I want to . . . still."

Then Angela screamed, a genuine howl of pain, not an act, Eddie was sure of it. "God damn you, Corey!" she wailed, rushing at the stage. "God damn you!" she hollered again just as she tripped and threw herself headlong down the steeply sloping aisle. Her father stood up as she landed hard. Then Eddie saw Crenshaw leap from the shadows and come to her aid. She was crying uncontrollably, her head and shoulders shaking, her breath coming in staggering gasps.

Crenshaw put his powerful arms around her and helped her to her feet. All the fight had gone out of her, and she slumped against him and sobbed into his shirt. Both Crenshaw and Eddie looked back to the stage in time to see R. Todd Favor swivel his neck and pull at his shirt collar. He took one step toward Angela, and said something; Eddie couldn't hear what. Crenshaw looked over and waved him offstage. R. Todd Favor winced and sagged visibly but held his ground for another few seconds. Then he squared his shoulders, adjusted his tie, and began his exit. Before disappearing in the shadows, he looked again at his daughter and reached out with his left hand, as if to explain something. But there was no last saving word from R. Todd Favor. Finally he left the stage.

Down in the aisle, Eddie could hear Crenshaw saying, "There now, Angela. You'll be all right. There now, honey."

chapter 19

She's at Hennepin County Medical Center," Crenshaw was saying from behind his desk. "In the psych ward, under sedation."

"Did she admit anything yet?" asked Roger Doyle, the only parent present in the small group seated before Crenshaw.

"Not exactly."

"What's that mean?"

"She's making allusions to the crime but speaking in images."

"When she calms down," commented McDowell, "when she feels safer and a little more secure, I'm confident she'll clarify a good deal for us. You see, there's no reason to hide it anymore. She's virtually gone public with her rage already."

Eddie sat off to the side, thinking, If this guy goes on much longer, talking that talk, we'll all be lost again. ACE stood behind Eddie, her hand on his shoulder.

"Tell you what I think," continued Crenshaw, "the girl is a certifiable genius. If she'd *never* said anything, given herself away. . ."

Eddie watched the psychiatrist McDowell nod, but Roger Doyle looked down at his own folded hands, giving no indication that he followed Crenshaw's reasoning. Maybe he didn't have to, thought Eddie.

Just then Doyle stood up, thanked Crenshaw again for his efforts, and excused himself. McDowell followed him out of the room.

Alone with Crenshaw and Cynthia, Eddie wanted to ask Crenshaw how he was able to get R. Todd Favor to be the main act in Angela's psychodrama. But before he could inquire, Crenshaw said, "Any other questions?"

Eddie blurted, "Angela's father."

"Uh-huh, what about him?" Crenshaw said pleasantly.

"Well, how'd you convince him to go along? I mean, wouldn't he, being a lawyer and all, want to fight for her?" Stand up for her, thought Eddie.

"You know what? She was almost on the money about him. After I talked to the guy, he was scared. He said he knew what Angela's capable of doing. So he agreed to help to save his daughter and to save his image by getting her put away. It didn't take long to convince him we had enough for a case. And he realized that if we just went to trial, the initial publicity alone would be more damaging than a conviction to his reputation and any future she might have. So it's not like he doesn't care. It was a big risk for him to go onstage. Maybe he doesn't know how to care enough, something like that."

"But it worked to bring him in," Eddie concluded.

"You mean we got her."

"Yeah."

"Well, I won't say it worked or didn't work till everything shakes itself out. At least she's getting some help."

Eddie remained silent.

Cynthia ended it with, "We all appreciate how well this was handled, Detective. Thank you from us." She patted Eddie's shoulder.

"Yeah," Eddie concurred, standing up now.

"You're the man," Crenshaw said to Eddie. "You did the right thing when it made a difference to do the right thing, and in this business good timing is pretty much the whole show." Then Crenshaw stood up and reached his right hand across the desk. "You did *real* good, Edrich," he said, shaking Eddie's hand. "Now go home and make yourself do school and everything else as well as you've done this."

Eddie smiled and gave Crenshaw a nod. And he meant it. He'd go back to Nicollet and make the best of it. He'd try to take school and himself seriously. He would try to make a self there that he could hang on to. In fact, he couldn't wait to hear more of the truth according to Goldman, couldn't wait to play ball again. Everything looked good just now, because he'd followed his instincts and they'd been good.

He wouldn't ever forget Angela, all she'd shown

him in the short time they were together. For despite their superficial differences, they had much in common. Through her Eddie had seen all too clearly what can happen when you don't take time to face your own anger, when you let it control you, when you let anger become rage.

As he turned to leave, Cynthia took his arm, leaned close, and said, "He's right, Eddie."

Eddie gave her a questioning look.

"You should go home."

Eddie flinched, pulled back a little.

Cynthia read him perfectly.

"With me," she clarified. "Home."